THE WITCH
OF
MONROE

ALSO BY TRACE MURILLO

The Patient in Room 432
A Girl Named Carmen Winstead

COMING SOON
The Wendigo
Whispering Creek

THE WITCH OF MONROE

TRACE MURILLO

Published by Dark Water Press, LLC
Trademarks of Dark Water Press.

ISBN-13: 9781737068341
ISBN-10: 1737068341
Cover design by Emily's World of Design
Interior formatting by Todd Keisling | Dullington Design Co.
Editor: Eleanor Ransburg

Library of Congress Control Number: 2022910389

876543

Printed in the United States of America

The devil doesn't come dressed in a red cape and pointy horns. He comes as everything you've ever wished for.

—*Tucker Max*

For Joshua, your love and knowledge of everything, *is inspiring.*
My real-life hero.

THE WITCH OF MONROE

CHAPTER I

In the gloom of dusk, Lawrence Hovey let out a curse as he watched the rabbit leap into the underbrush. Lawrence, called "Captain" by most who knew him, leveled his rifle and nearly fired a shot out of sheer frustration. But that would have been a waste of gunpowder, and Lord only knew his supplies were dwindling. Also, it was a fool's errand to fire a shot and not hit anything.

He supposed he was responsible for his own frustrations. He had been walking around the forest for a while and had even thought about calling it a day, but his stomach was growling like a lone wolf. Right before he'd noticed the rabbit, he was thinking he'd be perfectly happy with whatever Hannah could manage to scrape together: something out of their garden, and the bit of venison they had left from last week's hunt. But for about a week now, he'd been craving rabbit stew — a dish his own mother had perfected in a pot over the fire at the hearth of his boyhood home.

Lately, Captain had been thinking a lot about that childhood home. He had been thinking of his mother, a godly woman who had safely brought six children into the world before she died giving birth to the seventh. Captain thought of his mother from time to time and cherished his childhood memories, even the tough times they'd had. For reasons he did not understand, the memories had been quite pressing for the last few days.

That's why he currently found himself in these damned Connecticut woods, looking for a hare at just about sundown. He had told Hannah, who was waiting back home, to get the fire ready and a stew started. What he had not told her was that, after dinner, he intended to have her as a man desires a wife. She had not been agreeable to it as of late and that was fine, he knew she had been feeling unwell, something to do with the bone aches of her hands. He understood her pains and would never force himself on her, but Hannah being twenty years his junior made him think it was time they started to have children, and this night he would not be denied whether she was in pain or not. So, thinking the hare would make some sort of romantic gesture, he was determined not to go home empty-handed.

Captain hunkered down among the vines and briars,

looking into the thicket the rabbit had disappeared into. It had the look and feel of a den, dark and cold on the inside. The hare he had just missed had been a small one. *Certainly*, he thought, *there was a mother or father hare lurking behind to make sure all the children made it home.* The parents were the ones he wanted, so he waited. He felt his body shiver as dusk morphed into night. Rabbits weren't usually keen to wander around in the dark. He knew it was only a matter of time.

Sure enough, he heard something moving in the brush to his right, just beyond a grove of tall hickories. His eyes widened as he turned his head the slightest bit, waiting to see the motion so he could time his shot just right. He knew if he moved, it could throw his posture and sight off. So, he waited, a rather skilled marksman trusting his instincts.

But when the shape came out of the brush, it was not a rabbit, but something much larger. Captain saw a foot, clad in a dusty boot, the heel well-worn. He tried to look up at the intruder, supposing it might be one of his neighbors also out for a hunt. Maybe Rube Nichols, still convinced that deer came out just shy of dark, something they had debated many times while sharing tumblers of whiskey. Captain always shook his head at the man, often wondering how his family even survived the harsh winters with Rube thinking such nonsense. But when he tried to move his head, Captain found that his entire body was frozen. He could not move his neck or his hands. It even became difficult to draw air into his lungs, and the air he did take in felt frigid and cold with no meaning to it at all.

He heard the boot step closer, then a second one sliding along the brush beside it. A shadow fell over Captain, and the world grew even colder and darker. But still, he could not move. It was a paralysis he could feel sinking into him and wrapping itself deep down around his bones.

"Am I bewitched?" he asked the figure he could not see.

"Mayhap," came the answer. It was a man's voice, but it was sweet as honey. Captain was again reminded of his childhood; of rhymes and stories his father had shared as they searched for bee shelters to steal the honey. This was before the man had taken his own life. It was a memory Captain had long forgot.

"I serve the Lord," Captain Hovey said in a tone that was meant for authority but possessed very little. "No demon holds sway over me."

"You speak the truth," the man said. "But other things may grasp you. These woods, for instance. The creatures in it. The vegetation. You reap it, you kill it, you claim it as your own, yes?"

Captain had no idea how to answer. His hands still clutched the rifle, but he could not move an inch. It was more than the deadness of his movements. Now it felt like there was ice being sewn into his skin. It burned, and his nostrils were tinged by the smell of smoke wafting up as something turned to ash.

"Are you a devil, sir?" Captain asked, no longer trying to sound defensive.

The man chuckled. "There are no devils," he said. Then, with a sigh that made Captain assume this man had a face as beautiful as his voice, the unseen figure moved closer.

"You wish to be rid of me, yes?"

"Yes. Turn away from me, devil."

"There are no devils," it said again.

The bottom of the figure's long black cloak came into view. Captain watched it carefully as it began to sway with the slight sound of the wind. Then he heard a clicking noise when it snapped its fingers. The cloaked stopped dancing, lodged in time as the ice in Captain Hovey's body thawed at once and he was able to move again. His first instinct was to swivel the rifle around and blast a hole in whatever godless being had dared trespass in the woods of a God-fearing man, but fear had taken over, and he remained compelled. The figure snapped again, and Captain felt himself being pulled off the ground, levitating from whatever hold the figure had over him. He felt a scream developing in his throat, but it came out as a soft cry that made the figure giggle slightly as Captain felt his feet land back on solid earth. He dropped his rifle and noticed his foot stepping forward, realizing he had no control over his body when he stepped again and felt like he was being pushed forward by something he could not see. He trampled through where he thought the rabbit den to be and tore through the forest beyond, begging his body to stop, but it would not listen. He was only a passenger, and his rebelling body was the carriage.

His legs pumped and his knees bent, but he did not send the commands. It was as if he were outside his own body, unable to control himself. His lungs burned as he drew a long breath and let out a low-pitched moan. There was nothing more he could do as he felt the forces pushing him deeper and deeper into the night. *The devil*, he whispered.

There are no devils. He heard the beautiful voice scream in his head.

Captain Hovey knew where he was headed, and a dread as sharp as nails tore into his heart. Wayman's Gorge was just up ahead, a fifty-foot drop into a dried-up creek bed. When the land had been discovered, there had been the remains of decayed villages: little abodes, scattered weapons, and fragments of their bodies all wasted away.

Branches slapped at his face. He felt the burning as his flesh was ripped from his skin. When he tried to cry out to God to rebuke whatever devil had a hold on him, he discovered that he didn't even have control over his own thoughts. The prayers fell dead to the floor of his mind as Wayman's Gorge drew closer and closer.

Captain noticed the dancing shadows of the lined cypresses that stood stoic like guardians on each side of him. As he moved swiftly, deeper and deeper into the darkness, the forest became more evident, swaying off the reflection of the moon. There was no other movement, not even the shapes of the rabbits he was just hunting or the deer that Rube Nichols claimed fed there when the sun went down. There was nothing, and when his right foot extended forward and found only open air, Captain was alone. The only thing that was there was the gorge that waited for him below. It was mostly shrouded in darkness. He thought he could feel the creature with the beautiful voice falling beside him, smiling. For a moment, Captain felt safe, as if the creature had taken away all his worries, all of his sins. Then images danced in his mind like flickering beeswax. He saw his dad, caressing bees, licking the welts of his stings, sucking the venom, his bone and flesh exposed. Then his mom, cooking rabbit stew over her hearth, the rabbits screaming into the night as she lowered them into the hot boiling water, their claws slashing at her skin. Then the image changed again. It was like flashes of light awakened his mind. He saw Hannah, his beautiful, sweet Hannah. She lay on the bed of the forest laughing, her long dark hair extended out like a crowned veil around the bottom of the trees. Twisted roots dipped in and out of the ground. The distorted branches reached down like fingers, grasping her skin. Hannah caressed her plump breast, moving her fingers toward her toned thighs as snakes slithered up, enjoying her pale flesh. And as he fell, whispers filled his ears.

"See…I told you, there are no devils."

CHAPTER 2

Hannah watched from the kitchen window as the two boys from town tiptoed toward the dirt track that led to her lawn. One of the boys inched closer, while the other eyed the house. They were both giggling in a happy and nervous sort of way. Hannah did not think there was any fear to them at all. No, they were only here because it now seemed to be an obligation that the boys of Trumbull get as close to the fabled home of Hannah Hovey as they could—though for reasons unknown to her, they had started referring to her as Hannah Cranna. At that moment, she figured those chattering boys were daring one another to venture as close as they could. Something she could only imagine.

After Captain's funeral, she knew it was going to be bad. No one in Trumbull had ever really cared for her. Some of the more noble women believed she had not deserved Captain—that he had only settled for her because of her youth and beauty. Others claimed it was because of her somewhat exotic past. Some even called him a beard splitter for taking up with such a godless woman. The biggest issue in Trumbull for Hannah was that she was not a local, not even from this fledgling little state. No one really knew where she had come from, and as far as they were concerned, that was an automatic mark against her.

As the pastor recited scripture from the Good Book over the pine box that held Captain's body, Hannah had felt their eyes on her, followed by the whispers. It felt like fire piercing her soul, burning deep within, though she ignored it as she watched them lower Captain's body into its final resting spot. But even before Captain had been fit and sized for his coffin, Hannah knew the stories had begun to spread.

She had heard them all. When she was alone, especially on the quiet nights without even a bird chirp or an owl hoot, on those nights when the sun went to sleep and the moon turned its face from Trumbull, Hannah would lie in her bed playing the scenarios out in her head, trying to understand why the townspeople would spin such yarns.

"*She murdered him somehow. It was Hannah Cranna who caused Captain to fall to his death. An experienced woodsman such as he would never die in such a way!*"

"*She was a witch. She had cursed him or driven some*

demon of the wilderness into his Christian heart. Surely, she was a witch. Why else would such a pretty woman stay so secretive about her past?"

There was also the idea that Captain had committed suicide. Realizing his error in marrying such a wayward and often odd woman had caused the poor man to throw himself off Wayman's Gorge. *It was just his guilt for going against God.* Hannah smiled at this one.

Hannah did her best to keep the memories at bay, except on occasion they would come on like stars shooting across the nights sky. Loose and on their own. In some ways, Hannah figured it was the creative process of being a widow. She watched those daring boys just at the edge of the yard and wondered if they had certainly heard some of the tales. A spiteful and fun-seeking part of Hannah wanted to go to the front door, open it and peer out and send the boys racing back to town to tell everyone they had seen that cursed old bitch Hannah Cranna. Had it been any other day, she might have done that very thing.

Today, though, for some reason, she was feeling the loss of Captain harder than she had in the nine days since his death. She never thought she would miss him so much. Maybe it was because she had finally forced herself to look through the closet and the old, scarred bureau he'd kept his clothes in. Maybe it was because she was now alone, a widow. She wasn't sure, but she knew he would want his belongings distributed to those less fortunate—of which there were many in Trumbull.

Hannah had packed up his stuff with delight, trying to keep Captain's secrets away from prying eyes. Everyone knew Captain, but there were two sides of him. There was the side that served the lord and the parish with delight. He even brought many ideas to Trumbull and even made a very comfortable life for himself on the outskirts of town thanks to his successful lumber business. He also served as a consultant on where to properly plant tobacco for the richest harvest. Last Spring, some folks from Virginia come up to visit him, causing quite the stir in town. But Captain assured them, it was for more businesses to move in and nothing more. Then there was the Captain that Hannah knew. The hard-handed man that was not so kind and demanded everything from her.

She had placed his Sunday suits and the few pieces of ornate China from his mother on their bed, returning her attention to this sad work while ignoring the boys and remembering the undertakers visit two days prior. He had stopped by with the boots Captain had been wearing when he died, as well as the watch he'd kept in the pocket of whatever vest he was wearing. The man had explained in a very churlish way, standing on her porch, and not making eye contact with her, that Captain's shirt had been ruined. He did not say as much, but she assumed it was because it had caught most of the blood. From what she had been told, and not very gently, her husband's head had been unsalvageable from the fall, and his spine and ribs had been little more than chunks and powder.

She looked at the boots, picking them up with curiosity. She examined the soles, the tread, wondering what it had been like and wishing she had seen him fall. The tread was barely worn in since the boots were relatively new. The smell of the leather, mingled with dirt and sweat, entered her nostrils, the scent of a hard-working man still lingering within them. The thought brought a lump to her throat, and she felt her eyes fill with tears. She sat the boots aside, sniffled back her emotions, and checked the watch next. She knew it had survived the fall, for she had checked it about twenty times since the undertaker had dropped it off along with the billfold and the small amount of money it had inside.

Now, as she opened the watch, it continued to tick away the seconds of the afternoon. She closed her eyes, held it to her ear, and listened. She felt the ticking like a heartbeat, and, for a moment, she sensed that Captain was there with her. The cabin felt like that from time to time. She could feel him as she wept in the kitchen, or when she sat in their bedroom rubbing milk lotion on her skin or as she tried her best to go to sleep in the bed that now felt very lonely and too big just for Hannah.

A single tear finally escaped, and she wiped it away quickly. Her hands began shaking slightly when she set the pocket watch down with the rest of his belongings and caressed them gently. Hannah thought she had seen him everywhere in the cabin over the last few days. Shadows of him anyway. Standing in the corners of the kitchen as she cooked over the hearth, a feeling of him as she watched the shadows of the moon bounce across the walls as she lay, tossing and turning, impatient for sleep to come. Mostly she brushed it off as grief, yet the specter of him remained, haunting her, mocking her, making her question herself as the memories continued to pull her in and out of reality.

Suddenly the chattering and laughter of the boys just outside her yard broke into her thoughts. She sauntered toward the window and slowly raised her hand to pull back the burlap that covered the opening. She did this just in time to see the last bit of their fun as one of them unabashedly dropped his pants and urinated in her yard. Hannah noticed that the taller of the boys, no more than ten years old, dressed in a white tunic and black knee pants, had seen her peering at them. She noticed he was shaking slightly when he raised his finger, pointed, and began screaming, *"You're a witch! You're a witch! Hannah Cranna is a goddamn witch!"* Hannah felt her heart sink lower than it had felt when she was going through Captain's belongings. Letting her hand fall away from the curtain, she walked back to the bed and sat down.

She shut her eyes and took a few deep breaths as the room went dark. She wanted to shut out the world that was circling around her. The voices were becoming deafening, the memories taunting, and Hannah just wanted them to stop. But it was no use, everything was just a realistic replay of the day Captain died. Then it morphed into something more sinister: the wind blowing all around her, the serpents coiling on her skin. The bloody smell of Captain had never completely left the back of her throat. Sometimes it grew into a hot, choking torrent, a coppery flood that filled her mouth and nostrils and drowned her thoughts. She jerked out of the notions, wrenched her mind back to the present, puttering and somewhat breathless as she shook off the image of Captain's body laid out on the back of Rube Nichols' carriage.

CHAPTER 3

A small carriage arrived at the cabin shortly before sundown. Drawn by two horses, it was driven by a member of Holy Hearts Lutheran Parish. Hannah watched from the window and noticed a tall, sour-looking man climbing down from the carriage; it was like watching a raccoon clamber down a tree. He approached the cabin slowly, eyeing it as if he feared it might burst into flames at any moment. Hannah noticed how he clutched his Bible tightly to his chest.

Once the man stepped onto the porch, he seemed to move a little faster, and when he had physically touched the house, Hannah assumed he wanted his business done as soon as possible. She heard his feet pound hard at the wood slats Captain had replaced the previous summer, but when he came to the door, he knocked as gently as a bird. Hannah answered right away, leaning one hand on the frame and gently resting the other on her hip. She was rightly surprised when she saw Pastor Dunne standing there with a smile that seemed genuine. What she was not surprised about was how it seemed to take him a moment to find his tongue. She had long ago gotten accustomed to men finding themselves in awe of her. Her beauty was alluring, though she tried to never think of herself as such. Her mother had told her repeatedly that her beauty was of the devil and that there would be plenty of male suitors who would have no problem partaking in such evils. Some would even go mad with their desire for her, but Hannah always thought of herself as a charmer and nothing more.

Apparently, it was a charm that even pastors were not immune to, and she wondered if this might be one of the reasons many of her neighbors now thought of her as something less than traditional. "*Have you come to bewitch us all?*" In the puritan tradition, she assumed that was the first question asked to outsiders who looked like Hannah, but she wasn't sure.

"Ms. Hovey how are you?" he asked, staring at the long dark locks draping over her breasts—then blushing once he realized Hannah had noticed. She tilted her head, and her red tinted lips slipped a little, making Pastor Dunne quickly look at the floor. Hannah reined it in, but it wasn't easy. She didn't want to show an expression of anything more than a widowed woman, still in mourning.

"Much better these days, thank you, Pastor." Hannah guided him toward the kitchen table, feeling the heat of the fire stove she had been running all day. It was good to hear someone refer to her by her actual name. She wasn't sure what *Hannah Cranna* meant, but she did not like it. She felt that, even if it were the creation of bored children, there was a veiled insult in there somewhere.

"It is a very noble thing what you are doing, giving Captain's belongings to those in need," Pastor Dunne said, removing his black bowler hat and setting it on the table. "Matter of fact, there's a young man getting married in a few days who can't afford a decent suit. He's about Captain's size, I'd imagine..." Hannah could tell the pastor was nervous as he continued babbling about people in Trumbull who could use Captain's things. He continued to stare at the floor around the room, at the walls, at the door...anywhere but at Hannah. She assumed he didn't want his eyes to wander anymore, so she moved across the room and added another log on the hearth.

"That would be wonderful," Hannah said as the sparks of the fire speckled the room. "I'm sure Captain would be truly happy for his clothes to be used in such a way."

"I take it these are the sacks?" Pastor Dunne nodded toward the two grain sacks she had packed up and set against the wall of the den. Deep down, it hurt her to realize that they held most of the earthly belongings Captain had left behind.

"Yes, let me give you a hand," she said, walking toward them.

"Thank you kindly. But before we get to that, there's something I'd like to ask you."

She had expected this, and honestly, she didn't really mind. She supposed it showed that at least some people in town gave a damn about her. When Pastor Dunne spoke, she found that her suspicion had been right.

"There are some rumors, Mrs. Hovey. It is of wickedness, and I am here to ask for the men of God in this town if there are truths to be had?"

"Wickedness? No, sir," she said, trying to hide her scorn. "There is no wickedness from me. I honestly don't know where it all came from. It seems to me that as soon as Captain died, the people in town saw fit to just assume certain things about me."

"We are God-fearing people—God-fearing *women,* to be more accurate in your situation. Well, I hope anyway. You came into town out of nowhere and, within six months, picked up the town's most notable and well-known gentleman. And as a happily married man to a literal angel on earth, I feel confident in telling you that you have a look about you as well. You're different from the other women around here. It also does not help that the much-wanted God-fearing man who married you, by his own admission I might add, claimed he would likely never take a shine to marriage. Well, the women got jealous, and their menfolk pacified them. It isn't godly at all, but I can understand it, I suppose. And that is why we must pray to our Lord and Savior for forgiveness."

"I suppose," Hannah echoed. "But I will not be praying to your Lord and Savior today, Pastor."

"Mrs. Hovey, that is blasphemy! Do you not know about salvation through our Lord Jesus Christ?"

"I know of it, yes, of course."

"And do you hold stock in it?" Pastor Dunne asked, finally making eye contact with Hannah. "Have you repented of your sinful nature and given your life to Him?"

"I don't take stock in anything, Pastor, and I can't say that I have given my life to anyone." Hannah realized the pastor was bothered by what she was saying.

"I will be honored and happy to show you how, Mrs. Hovey," he said, leaning forward eagerly. "It is not difficult. Our Lord and Savior is very understanding." It was as if he had cast a lure into a river and knew the fish were about to bite.

"I appreciate the effort, but like I said, not today. Not in my sorrow. Not in my grief."

Pastor Dunne took a step away from Hannah and narrowed his eyes at her. "There is no better time to turn your eyes and heart to Almighty God than in a time of grief, my child. He can take that sorrow and grief from you like a thief that comes into your home and steals away your bread."

"Mayhap He can," Hannah said. "But to give my life to another man so soon after losing such a good one seems foolish, doesn't it? And if it is an eternal decision I'll be making, I'd rather do it with a heart and mind not weighed down by sorrow."

Pastor Dunne had been on the verge of opening his Bible, but his hands now froze and clutched the book tightly. "Such talk won't do much to do away with the errors of this town," he said. "Such talk will be echoed through the meeting house of God and ricochet off the hearts that all divulge in His word."

"Now, you wouldn't be adding any kindling to those rumors when you leave here, would you, Pastor?" Hannah said, leaning closer to him and allowing her long black-sleeved bustier to trickle down over her left shoulder. Her brilliant golden eyes shot through him like lightning.

Pastor Dunne turned his head away quickly and relaxed his posture, no longer looking like a fisherman but a man who had been insulted. He started for the grain sacks that held Captain's belongings, and when Hannah tried to help him, Pastor Dunne shook his head. "I believe I can manage, Mrs. Hovey," he said, without looking at her. "Thank you kindly."

She watched him struggle with carrying both sacks and his Bible, but knew better than to offer her help again, choosing instead to watch him cross the lawn and toss the sacks into the carriage as if they were nothing more than old, soiled laundry. After climbing back up behind the reins, the pastor gave the cabin a final furtive glance and turned the horse around. Hannah smiled when she realized that even the horse had a bit of speed in its step, just as anxious to get away from the cabin as Pastor Dunne seemed to be.

CHAPTER 4

Not long after Pastor Dunne had come by to get Captain's belongings, the fall season, which had settled in about two weeks before, truly announced itself with the first honestly cold night. Hannah awoke with a fire of agony in both hands. She had been told that joint pains of the kind she suffered were usually not experienced until the age of forty or so—maybe thirty in men who constantly used their hands for grueling manual labor. The Trumbull doctor had referred to her joint pains as *rheumatism* and claimed she had one of the worst cases he had ever seen. When asked about why her hands were so gnarled and bizarre, Hannah had feigned ignorance, though she was quite sure the doctor knew she was lying. Hands like hers couldn't be so mangled without someone with experience being able to pull a story from them.

Hannah got up from her feathered mattress and lit her spermaceti candle. She watched the light dance across the cabin walls, leaving a thin reflection of shadows flickering around the darkened room. The flame was small, but it was enough light for Hannah as she moved slowly past the hearth and set the candle on the table. She rubbed her hands near the heat, hoping the pain would subside. She pulled the Boston rocker, a chair that Captain had picked up on one of his many trips to Virginia, closer to the hearth, and in the weak candlelight of that first chilly fall night, Hannah sat there rocking, recalling the reason for the state of her pains quite well. She saw her mother's face and the large hammer held tightly in her callused hands. She remembered her mother's fingers moving around the handle as if she were playing a Renaissance harp on a Sunday morning, but this was no harp, and when her mother brought the hammer down, the pain was unbearable. Hannah remembered being drawn into the darkness. The sweet forgetfulness of the memory made it hard to remember the exact pain. She knew it had hurt much worse than the current aches chewing through her bones and was grateful she could not fathom the extent of it.

Making a grimace while she gently massaged her hands, Hannah wondered how long her small store of firewood would last. There were a few stray logs in the barn, probably enough to heat the cabin for two days, but that was it. Captain had sold a big chunk of his supply to the mercantile store before he died, and never had a chance to replicate his stash. Hannah figured she would have to split her own. She was perfectly capable of doing it and had done it before, but that had been in warmer weather, when her hands weren't singing holy hell.

"I'll fight that burden when it bites me," she said as she rose from the rocker and grabbed the old lantern. She slipped on her house shoes and night jacket and headed outside.

She was grateful the moon was nearly half full. It gave her ample light as she walked around to the back of the house. She couldn't remember if she had ever seen the flat and featureless back yard at night because, normally, fetching more firewood was Captain's job. But now that she was alone, this task was something she would have to get used to. Hannah looked around the yard, swinging the lantern from side to side. Suddenly an old childhood fear of the night began to build up, but she pushed it aside. She knew that if she didn't get some wood for the fire to keep her hands warm, the pain would cause her fingers to curl like skeletal bones.

Moving slowly toward the barn, deeper into the night, she watched the moon as it slowly began to abandon her. Specks of the dark clouds scurried away from the darkness, and she felt the fear creeping deeper and deeper into her soul. Finally, she noticed the barn where Captain typically kept a stack of firewood. It was roughly ten yards away from the back wall. Normally it would be fully stocked throughout the fall, winter, and even the earlier spring months, but now it was mostly empty, offering very little hope. She felt foolish for not having thought of this before the harsh weather settled in, but there was a good reason it had slipped her mind. She had been preoccupied with burying her husband and grieving his loss. Now she regretted it.

Hannah saw something glistening against the night and heard some sort of scrambling from the tree line that surrounded her property. She abruptly turned her head toward the sound and then back toward the barn, which made her long dark braid fall over her shoulder and her eyes widen. She felt relief fill her chest when she noticed Captain's ax leaning against the old threshing machine, he had never been able to part with. As she stared curiously at the old ax, she knew there was no way she would be able to properly grip it with her hands feeling as they did. She would not be able to cut the firewood. Even thinking about it made her hands want to curl in on themselves, and her knuckles bunched into knots. The darkness enveloped her like a cloak, and her stomach churned and went cold.

Hannah saw the wood stacked neatly against the wall. There wasn't much, so she settled for the few scraps left over from the previous season's pile. They were dried out and old, but they would burn just fine if she could get the flames started properly. There were five, maybe six pieces, though she could only carry three at a time. Even holding them close to her breast was enough to cause her hands to tremble in pain. She bit back a cry as she carried them into the cabin and let them roll out of her arms to land by the hearth with a loud *thunk*. She poked and prodded at the old wood still smoldering inside the hearth. Most of it had burned down to ash, but the logs that remained flared up. The escaping sparks flew around the cabin like a swarm of fireflies on a warm summer night. She added some kindling and worked on the coals to get a good fire going.

She had made fires before, but never with her hands hurting so badly. What truly scared her was that it wasn't all that cold yet, and if she was hurting like this right now, she could only imagine what it would be like come December and January. It took a while to get a respectable flame going, and once she did, she cautiously fed two little logs into it.

Hannah stared curiously as the fire caught. The crackling of the wood made her miss Captain. She remembered how they would lie next to the fire on cold winter nights, laughing and trying to stay warm. That was before everything went so wrong. That was the Captain she missed.

She knew the small flame would get her through the night, but she would have to go back to the barn for the rest of the wood for morning. Her hands felt as if they were burning inside, but she knew she had to do it. She went back out into the darkness, the moon still casting small shadows, hiding behind the mulberry and black birch trees that lined the surrounding forest. Her feet pounded against the path as she tried to flex the pain from her hands. As she moved quickly to where the last two pieces of wood remained, she saw the silhouette of a man standing just to the right of the barn door. For a moment, she was sure it was Captain—that he was visiting from whatever place existed beyond this one. Perhaps Pastor Dunne's fabled Heaven, or one of the Asian afterlife's she had once read about in an old charlatan rag.

"Law...Lawrence?"

Her voice shivered. She hadn't spoken his actual name in a very long time. Even at his funeral, very few people had uttered his Christian name, as he had been known as Captain since his boyhood. It wasn't until he'd married her that she learned his first name was Lawrence. To her, he had always been just Captain.

Before the name was completely out of her mouth, the figure was gone. She closed her eyes and took a deep breath. The air seemed thick and cool. As hysteria set in, Hannah felt tears fill her eyes. Her bottom lip quivered with uncertainty. She used all of her strength to push forward, and when she opened her eyes, she staggered a little, but the door by the barn remained empty. She moved faster, holding the lantern in front of her like a shield, hoping it would protect her from whatever was ahead. When she approached the barn, her night-shrouded eyes widened as the figure appeared again. Like Captain, the image morphed into an ashy dust, falling slowly to the ground, and disappearing into the night. Hannah felt a ball develop in her throat. Her nerves blocked her airway. Inhaling through her nostrils, she did her best to push it away, but her lungs felt constricted. A stream of bile developed, and she felt the burn as it bubbled up in her throat and bottomed out in her stomach. Her eyes widened even more as she slowly entered the barn and stopped. She looked around at the darkness of the structure, then back into the forest that surrounded her like a black circle. It seemed to have many layers, and the figure she saw seemed to have been wavering between two of them. Right where she stood, at the spot where she had thought she'd seen someone, there was no one now. Still, she sensed that something was there. Something was watching her and waiting.

Hannah blinked the image away and padded her way closer to the remaining pieces of wood. The last signs of what she had thought was a man disappeared. She quickly picked up the logs. Her body felt warm as she began to shake, and pain shot through her hands as if rusty metal was grinding into her bones. She cried out in agony. Not a scream of calling for help, just a visceral scream of outrage and disappointment damning her mother for the memories of what she had done.

Cradling the two pieces of wood against her chest, she heard it. A moan—so soft she wasn't certain she'd heard it at all. She froze, holding her breath, straining to hear. She anticipated the terror that had begun to prod at her. She fought against it and managed to push it back into the darkness that surrounded her.

She glanced quickly toward the forest, figuring it was the same thing she had heard earlier, maybe a wild animal or stray dog. It was far too easy for her mind to fetch up some imaginary things out there, but she continued tracing the edge of the property along the tree line with her eyes. At one point, she even imagined it was more of those damn neighborhood boys, coming to do more than just piss in her yard. All she knew was that the forest seemed to be alive with voices of malice, and she could not determine what any of them were.

Hannah turned from the forest and walked a few steps toward the house. The wind picked up slightly and ripped against her skin. It was cold, colder than it had been earlier and colder than it should be. The night was tightening its grip around her, and she felt it. Hannah remained hopeful, though. *Maybe it was all in her mind*, she thought. But then the sound of dead foliage broke behind her. It was footsteps.

Hannah knew something was there. She felt it. She closed her eyes and inhaled quickly. The feeling was strong, stronger than she had ever felt. The cool air took her breath as she paused, a wave of panic rising inside her. She opened her mouth to scream, but nothing escaped. She wanted to strike out at her tormentor, but none of her muscles obeyed her commands. Her chest felt constricted, but she gave a silent sigh. She searched again, knowing that somewhere in the darkness from the limits of her vision, there was something...someone.

Instantly, Hannah felt the hold on her slowly release and she hurried her step to the front yard, casting her eyes from side to side, but never turning around. With the remainder of the wood still tight in her grip, she made a lumbering step onto the porch, bypassing both stairs in her haste. She listened as the whispering began, soft sounds that seemed like words but were muddled in her ear. It was barely there, but she heard it. Another cry rose in her throat as she turned, staring out into the night. The trees looked like skeletal statues, ready to reach out like fingers scratching at her. Finally, a gust of wind threatened to take her as it pushed her back against the door, and the whisper came again.

A whisper, just a single word in the night, and she heard it this time.

"Hannah."

She fumbled with the handle on the door and pushed her way in. The whisper of voices grew to an incoherent babble, then a strange sucking sound, like a kitten drawing milk from its mother's teat. She dropped the wood on the floor and threw the bolt in its casing, locking the door as she leaned against the rotting wood. She inhaled slowly, and a sigh of relief escaped her mouth.

As she shuffled back to the safety of her bed, the whisper remained in her head, skittering across the floor of her mind, and pushing along the grit and leaves of her dreams.

"Hannah."

CHAPTER 5

The fire had dwindled down to hot coals by the time Hannah made her way out of her bedroom and toward the kitchen to make her morning brew. The cabin did not have that frigid chill yet, but she knew it would seep into her bones soon enough. This made her think of her hands. Staring down at them, she figured they were tolerable now, the pain from last night had almost completely faded, but the crisp air told her what the rest of the day would bring. Once it started to get cold in this part of the country, it stayed cold for a while.

January could be as cruel as a horrible beast. Some mornings, when Captain was still alive, it had been so cold that they would decide to not even get out of bed. They would stay under the blankets for most of the day, finding creative ways to keep each other warm. Thinking back, Hannah gave a sad smile–– those were the little moments Hannah missed the most now that Captain was gone.

She pulled herself out of those thoughts. "It's just you now," she whispered as she stoked the fire and carefully set the two pieces of wood into the embers. She closed the stove and set about making breakfast. It was a lonely affair, cooking her two eggs and letting her oats soak in water, but somehow, eating alone was worse. As she spooned the cold oats into her mouth, she dimly thought of the figure she thought she had seen the night before—the face, the movement out in the woods, and the whispering of her name.

He came, she thought. But in the light of day, it was quite easy to believe such things, convincing herself she might know about the visitor in the darkness. She shook the thought as the last of the discomfort started to fade from her hands. She flexed her fingers slowly and as she finished the last of her oats, she was relieved to find that they barely hurt at all. Hannah got up from the table and walked over to the apron sink Captain had welded for her a few years back and began washing her dish in the bin that rested securely inside. Her nerves crawled beneath her skin as she thought about the firewood again. Maybe if she could manage to get a healthy supply of firewood, she could avoid a painful winter. But given how the fine folks of Trumbull had decided she was some sort of witch, that might be easier said than done.

This thought tugged on her for a bit. Considering the last conversation she had with Pastor Dunne and remembering how the kids had peed on her lawn, she figured no one was likely to help her. She would just have to get it done herself.

She rummaged through one of Captain's drawers in the bureau, slowly pushing aside a few items she had not been able to part with—the deerskin coat he had looked so handsome in, the cotton shirt he had always preferred to wear to bed, stained with Hannah's own blood, the odd-looking cap that had been passed down from Captain's own father. She figured one day, and very soon, she would burn them herself. She finally came to what she was looking for: Captain's old, well-worn work gloves. She slipped one of them on and was reminded of just how big his hands were—not that she could ever forget. She removed the glove and stared at them closely, remembering his hands hard at work, clasped in prayer, and moving softly over her breasts. She even recalled the sting as he'd slapped his hand violently across her cheek. She closed her eyes, feeling Captain's arms around her, his warm breath on her neck, and his gentle fingers caressing her skin. She wanted to scream. But none of the old emotions were as keen as the sensation she felt right then. It aroused her. Remembering the pain Captain had sometimes caused, she moaned in delight—a moan that pulled her into the throes of ecstasy. She reached down and imagined it was the touch of him or the touch of anyone. It had been so long since

Hannah had been handled by a man, when her fingers trailed down her sculptured thighs underneath her house dress, she inhaled slightly and closed her eyes. It felt good. Her breast swelled instantly and hardened as her fingers tightened around them and pulled, elongating her nipples. Pulling and twisting, she felt the sensation all the way down as her legs shivered. Slowly, Hannah pushed her hands down into the black wool of pubic hair, and she felt herself open and go moist under her own touch. She moaned again, pushing two fingers deep inside, sliding them slowly in and out, tickling her clitoris in the process. Her thin white house dress fell off her shoulder exposing Hannah's soft skin, her dark nipples tingled as her breathing deepened, and she found herself in full euphoria.

Right before she was about to escape into full ecstasy, a loud thump at her door brought her back to reality and she realized it was not Captain in the thrills of her muff or the one that held her in comfort, but her own hands and the memories of her desires. With her eruption fading, she devolved into nothing more than an expression of pain and frustration—driving the last remnants of the memory from her consciousness. The arms that a moment ago had held her in comfort were suddenly a memory of dust, and the heat was nothing more than pain radiating from her hands. As Hannah looked around the room, breathing heavily, the room seemed just as lonely as she did.

Her lungs filled and expanded as the memory escaped, and she felt a slight lump in her throat as she lowered her gaze away from the trunk, adjusted her house dress, grabbed the gloves, and walked to the door. She knew she didn't have time to stand there desiring anyone or mourning for a man like Captain. Winter was fast approaching, and she figured she would have plenty of time for such issues. She abruptly opened the door, wondering who could be causing such a muck. Maybe the boys from Trumbull had moved from pissing on her lawn to throwing feces at her door. But Hannah's eyes widened as she stared across her yard. No one was there. She stared curiously toward the woods, then looked around the porch.

Small, muddy prints tracked across the floor. They were not normal prints. To Hannah, they looked more like talons, sharp claws, maybe skinny toes. They led from the end of her porch to her door. Hannah stood silent for a moment. The cool wind slapped towards the cabin. It felt ice-cold against her skin. Goose pimples dance up and down her arms. She embraced them with her hands, rubbing them slightly as she turned and walked back into the house.

Hannah glanced toward the single piece of wood sitting against the wall, then paced the room. She stared miserably at the mediocre fire inside the stove. Pulling at her white house dress in an involuntary twitch and clawing at her thighs, she stared curiously at the cupboards in the kitchen. She knew Captain had a fund in there, something she was never allowed to touch, but she figured he wouldn't mind now. After all, he would never allow his sweet Hannah to freeze to death, would he? She walked to the cupboard and plucked out the small candy tin in the back. When she opened it, it smelled sweet, just like Captain's favorite raspberry sugar, but the smell of the money Captain had hidden away inside was starting to overtake it. She gathered a few bills and a handful of coins and dropped them in the apron-like pockets of her house dress. She put the candy tin back into the cupboard, wondering how much longer she would have to depend on that little treasure to get by. The day after Captain's death, the bank had told her that there would be money coming her way, but there was paperwork and legal issues that had to be tended to first. She did not care, trusting that Captain had taken care of her in his last will and affairs.

Hannah walked into her room and dressed quickly, then donned her black cloak and left the house. She peered up the trail that led into town, wondering just how thick the rumors had grown. She knew if there were young boys brave enough to creep about her house for a thrill, she could only imagine how bad it might be in the parish. There was no telling how deep the well of rumors about her had grown thanks to those same women Pastor Dunne had mentioned during his visit.

For such a God-fearing town, Trumbull sure did have a whole lot of mean-spirited devils. Captain had always been her shield from it all. Without him, she wasn't sure if the town would tolerate her, much less manage to find some kindness to extend her way. Captain, a God-fearing man himself, had adhered to the teachings of the Good Book and its stories of love and tolerance. But Hannah believed in something else altogether. It had led to some interesting and passionate discussions when they'd first married, but after a while, Captain grew tired of Hannah's beliefs. While she did not have an issue believing that Jesus was an actual man who once walked the earth, the Bible that Captain believed in so fervently had been nothing more than a fairy tale to her.

Captain had always ignored the local murmurings about Hannah. He saw them as nothing more than the superstitious fears of a small-minded community that did not appreciate anyone who might think differently than they did. She supposed he understood the difference due to his studies of Salem, the mishaps of the Puritans, and the darkness that followed. But in Trumbull, the understandings of Captain did not flow over to the others in the town. With him gone now, she was sure she was an outcast in their eyes.

Hannah was truly hoping she wouldn't have to wander into the town proper, for she avoided it every chance she got. There were neighbors along the way, and many of them had greatly respected Captain. She had met them all and spoken to most of them, but there was no real relationship between them. As she made her way down her porch steps, with the coins jingling in her dress pockets, she hoped their fondness for Captain would extend to her.

The trail was worn and rutted out, not a terrible obstacle for someone walking into town but burdensome for a novice carriage driver. It was mostly used by folks on foot. The distance from the cabin to the town proper was a little longer than a mile, and four houses sat between her cabin and the first building going into town which was the church. The dusty road had been labeled Crow Trail by the locals for reasons she had never cared to learn. It fit, though; it was usually a dead little road, worn away by rain and heat and the occasional snowstorms in winter months. But walking down the trail made Hannah feel as if she were in some old forgotten stretch of woods—some place people had etched a road into and then abandoned. Tall pines and spruce trees flourished on one side, and large oaks and chestnuts filled the other, landscaping each of the cabins as she passed. The actual town, more than twenty homes from what she gathered, sat on the other side of Crow Trail on the little road that ran through it. It almost seemed as if Captain had chosen their cabin because the location kept them away from the prying eyes and spiteful mouths of the townsfolk.

She felt the feeling of isolation wash away when she passed by the Nichols property. Rube Nichols was the only blacksmith in town, and his wife was rumored to make the best pies in all of Trumbull—maybe in the entire county.

They had two children who were always laughing and singing. The oldest had just turned ten. When Hannah passed by their house, she saw one of the kids—the younger of the two girls—playing outside, chasing a squirrel with a stick. When she spotted Hannah, the girl dropped the stick, giggled, and ran inside quickly.

Let's hope that's not a sign of things to come, Hannah thought.

She wandered farther up the dusty trail, passing another house. This one belonged to an old, retired banker. From what Captain had told her, the man's wife had died giving birth to their sixth child many years ago. All his kids had grown up now. Three had died, and the other three had headed up to New York a year or so ago in search of riches and a better life, leaving their father behind. Hannah found herself sucking deep breaths of cold air into her lungs. A feeling of being old and lonely came over her and she wondered if that was how her life was going to be, now that Captain was gone. For a second, she wondered if the banker was just a lonely old man waiting to dry up and blow away in the cool breeze of Trumbull. She wondered if that was all that was left for her. A slight giggle escaped her lips as she thought about it and came to the third house.

She stopped and looked at it for a moment. This was the one she was interested in. Hannah had never been the best when it came to social niceties, so she had no idea if it would be improper to approach a man about a hired job so soon after losing her husband. Add to that the things people were saying about her in town, and it became an even more precarious situation.

She noticed the parched grass and wildflowers clinging to life in the yard. The flowers looked like cold twigs after a morning frost. It reminded her of a childhood game she used to play called Freeze, remaining stoic until the wind blew and then roll as far as you could until it stopped. The flowers were swaying with the slight breeze breaking in from the forest in front of them. Hannah gazed at the strange scene and felt a shiver pass through her as if the coldness of the scene understood. Her childhood memories were never the happiest ones and thinking of the man who lived here only drove the sadness deeper into her bones.

His name was Elmer Jefferson, and his wife was Sally. Hannah was quite sure they had children, but she did not know their ages or names. Captain had never mentioned it, but what he did mention was the coy attitude Elmer always portrayed and the many disagreements he and Captain often had at the saloon in town.

Hannah inhaled, flexed her fingers, took a step toward the porch, and stopped. She was anxious, and as nerves developed in her stomach, she remembered a promise she had made to herself after her mother had broken her hands with the hammer: Never ask anyone for help. She had simply lived a life trying her best and thinking that asking for any sort of help was a sign of weakness—an invitation for the world and the miserable creatures who lived in it to abuse you every chance they could. That is what Hannah thought and the rules she lived by. She was going to have to break that rule today, but she didn't know how to properly go about doing it.

Her heart was racing when she approached the porch. She noticed her hand shaking slightly as she started to knock, but the dark wooden door, blackened with age, opened before she could. Sally Jefferson was standing there with a fire poker in her hand raised like a sword in front of her, almost hitting Hannah. Sally, a frail woman, gazed at her with sightless eyes and a rigid look on her face. Hannah felt her body coil back and stood in silence for a moment until Sally spoke. Her voice was stern but frightened.

"Get on out of here, Hannah Cranna."

"I'm sorry to be a bother," Hannah said. "But I need some h—"

"I don't care what you need. Off you get. I can't be seen with no jezebel witch on my doorstep."

Hannah stumbled back and would have stepped away easily, but the mere confusion of the moment had left her frozen. Sally Jefferson, staring at her with those deep-set brown eyes, a homely woman that no one would ever look twice at in passing.

"What is it, woman?" a voice echoed behind Sally. Hannah felt a surge of fear, even worse than when Sally had opened the door a few seconds earlier. Elmer Jefferson stepped into view, placing a commanding hand on his wife's shoulder, and pushing her aside. His eyes landed on Hannah. A strange smile crossed his mouth, but it was immediately replaced by disgust.

"Hello, Mr. Jeff—"

"What in God's good name do you want, woman?" Elmer interrupted.

"With Captain gone, I need some help." She hated how weak she sounded, how desperate. That was simply not the sort of woman she was, never had been. Still, she could not bring herself to look the man in the eye as she went on. "Would you be able to help with firewood? I can pay y—"

"No," Elmer said. "We won't associate with you. And I won't take Captain Hovey's money."

"But I—"

"The answer is no. Now you go on, get off my land before I force you. If you're willing to pay for help, go into town. There's always some young buck around that needs money."

Hannah jumped as Elmer Jefferson slammed the door as if he were keeping the evil outside. She did not feel anger or sadness, just a deep sort of resentment. As she turned her back to the Jeffersons' cabin and made her way across the dead yard, it became abundantly clear to her that without

Captain around to serve as her spokesman, her image had gone back to the one she'd had to live down when she first appeared in town. Now, with local boys urinating in her yard and with neighbors unwilling to help her, it seems she was going to have to go into town after all—that or freeze this winter.

But no one really knew her, her beliefs, her goals. They only knew that she had come into town as a beautiful seventeen-year-old who never attended their dry and doom-filled church services. Captain had once described her arrival as something out of a fairy tale, where some goddess from another world came out of the woods of normal men, seeming strange, and in that beauty and strangeness, she was a threat.

She wasn't sure if the people of Trumbull would agree with that observation or not. All she knew was that, for some reason she did not understand, they all resented her for winning the heart of Captain Hovey, and now that he was gone, they had no reason to tolerate her any further. In fact, now that Captain was dead, it seemed they disliked her even more—which she assumed was where the rumors of witchcraft had come from.

I'll show them, she thought as she reached the trail again. She wondered if she should just go back home defeated or proceed into town. But the mere memory of the aching in her hands the night before caused her to turn to the right, toward Trumbull. With her head hung low and her dead husband's money making music in her pockets, Hannah Cranna headed into town like a whipped dog.

CHAPTER 6

She had never entered Trumbull alone. Anytime she'd ever walked into town, Captain had been with her. She was quite sure it was mainly because he enjoyed riling people up a bit and, according to Captain himself, he liked to show off what he referred to as "the prettiest lady in town." Walking off Crow Trail and into the main strip of Trumbull without him was harder than she thought. She knew it was foolish, but she thought she could feel every single eye on her, even eyes she could not see.

The first thing she saw as she crossed into Trumbull was the church. One of the oldest buildings in the area, it was showing its age. The wood slabs that stretched across the massive structure were beginning to crack, and the white paint that once might have been vibrant in color was blackened with grime and mold. There were a few children playing in the church yard, and an elderly woman with white hair and pale skin was rocking on the porch. Hannah nodded politely toward the woman, but immediately the woman yelled for the children to come inside. "Vixen," she heard the woman call out before she slammed the church door and shut Hannah out forever.

As she continued into the town proper, she was glad to see that there weren't many people out today. Normally there were many walking about. The women would gather whatever supplies their husbands told them to get while the men sat in the saloon drinking and making a muck out of everything. Church on Sundays, whiskey on Mondays. Hannah found that pretty ironic. The hypocrisy sometimes blew her mind. She did notice an old geezer sitting in a rocking chair on the porch of the general store. He immediately sat up when she passed by. His expression resembled a look as if a snake had reached up and bit him on his rear. His eyes as big as torpedoes as they settled on her. He said nothing, but his stare was enough of a statement.

There were a few people who milled through the streets, mostly men in dusty old suits. Every single one of them eyed her. Most showed disgust, though the younger ones had a bit of lustful interest in their stares. Finally, as Hannah passed the hotel, a middle-aged man with a well-trimmed mustache and a top hat that looked ridiculous on him gave her a simple

"Howdy, ma'am." Hannah returned the gesture with a smile. Then the man realized who she was and nearly collided with two children playing with a stick that had an old toad carcass attached to the end. Hannah's smile faded as the man took a wide step to the left and hurried on his way.

She scanned the streets, looking for someone who might be willing to help her. But there was no one. The trip to town wasn't a waste of her time though when Hannah remembered she was going to need to visit the pharmacy while she was there. She needed the tonic for her hands—the medicine Captain had brought to her in the past. It made her a little swimmy in the head, but it worked wonders. There was no way she was going to survive this winter without it.

As she walked toward the pharmacy, she noticed a man and a young boy, maybe his son, with a cart. They were parked between the sundry goods shop and the saloon. Their cart was loaded with neatly cut and stacked wood. Hannah could smell the freshness of it; it had always been among her favorite smells. She could see where some of their supply was missing; they had apparently sold quite a bit that morning.

Hannah eyed them for a moment, adjusted her bodice, then walked closer and stopped at the cart, hoping for kindness. The boy looked at her expectantly, but the father seemed very hesitant. His face wrenched up as if he had bitten into something sour before he managed to speak.

"Hello, Mrs. Hovey." It sounded like he was being strangled from the inside.

"Hello," she said as musically as she could. "I'd like to buy a load of your wood. Or maybe more, depending on the price," she explained, moving closer. In a way, her movement could be seen as a sharp contrast of her golden eyes and the sultry midnight hair that could be a powerful attraction to any man.

"My hands were broken long ago," she said in a smoky voice, "and I have too much pain to split my own." She almost added how it was a task Captain had always handled, but she did not want to use her dead husband as an excuse. Not among these people. Not yet anyway.

The father looked nervous, unable to find his voice. Hannah was quite sure she understood what had him so troubled. Maybe it was the combination of turning her away to save his reputation, or perhaps it was the mere thought of lust piercing his eyes.

"I-I don't know that I should be doing business with you," the man stuttered.

"And why is that?" Hannah leaned in, exposing her cleavage. "Why wouldn't you help a widow woman in need?"

The man's eyes grew large, and his jaw settled into a stern sort of sneer when he noticed his son watching him. "I've heard about you, Han-Hannah Cranna." The man began to studder.

"And what exactly have you heard, mister?" Hannah's eyes traced the man balefully, twirling her hair around her finger.

"Like you don't already know?"

"That's just the thing, sir. I truly don't." Hanna felt her heart begin to race, and the boy picked up on it as well. She watched as the child started to sway back and forth slightly, still smiling but a little anxious. Hannah noticed him staring up at her as if she were some strange beast from a foreign land. He continued to gape until Hannah winked at him, and he ran and hid between his father's legs. But on occasion, Hannah noticed the boy continued to peer at her— smiling.

"You will not help me?" Hannah turned toward the man who didn't seem to care that she was nothing more than a simple widow in need of help but was surrounded by selfish, miserable, so-called Christians who insisted on treating her like a leper and that was something she could not change.

"I will not take your money," the man said. Then he lowered his voice, looking both ways to make sure he was not going to be overheard. "But I do have some scrap wood back at my home that you can have. I'll have a boy bring it out to you, and you can pay him for the delivery." The man nervously removed his gloves and started to walk away from Hannah.

"But I have money to pay for *this* wood," she said, following him around the cart.

"I said, I do not want your money," the man said through

clenched teeth. She wished he was taking this stance because he wanted to help a widow, but she knew the real reason. He simply did not want to do business with her—not in the public eye, anyway.

"Well...I'll take it then. You know where it needs to be delivered to?"

"Aye, I know. Now please...walk away from us."

Hannah turned away and wondered if the man had simply lied to her to get her away or if he truly would have someone deliver the wood. She felt the man's eyes on her as she continued toward the pharmacy and smiled. She gripped her cloak around her body and thought she should be more bothered by the way she was being treated, that she should even be angry. But as it was, she found that she really didn't care. Without Captain around, she figured caring would make her old and wrinkled and she had no time for such things. But she also knew this could become a very dangerous mindset if she let it sink into her bones and consume her. She would never let them see her as the mean ole bitch Hannah Cranna they so often gossiped about. No, that would be dangerous.

As she made her way to the pharmacy, she passed a few more storefronts. Some were boarded up. Then she came upon a small building with a sign in the window that said, "Alterations." Hannah stopped and peered inside. Two old women were sitting in rockers, sewing hems, and making bobbins. Both women eyed her suspiciously and then went back to their tasks, sewing silk material for those in Trumbull who could afford it.

Suddenly, the smell of something rotten entered her nostrils. It was a small fruit stand nearby. It looked as if it hadn't been open since summer. Hannah walked around the stand and noticed a pair of women, walking closely in lockstep and eyeing her with unfiltered hostility. When Hannah's eyes met theirs, the women looked away quickly and sharpened their steps, almost tripping on their crinoline petticoats as they tightened their shawls around them. The soft cheeks of one of the ladies reddened considerably, almost as if she had been slapped by an invisible hand. Hannah smiled scornfully and finally approached the pharmacy.

Two old-timers were sitting on the front stoop. One had a bottle of brown whiskey in one hand and a long cigar in the other. He looked directly up at her when she walked to the door, grinned, and said, "Good day, witch."

"Careful," Hannah said as she opened the door and stopped. The man, shocked, looked up at her. His hands trembled as he struck a match on the ground and lit his cigar. She smiled fiendishly and walked into the pharmacy.

There were a few people scanning the goods on the shelves. Hannah kept her head low, wondering if they would just overlook her and pay her no mind. The pharmacy smelled musty and made her feel almost dizzy, but she stayed close to the walls and pretended to be interested in the items on the shelves. As she approached the back counter, the pharmacist—a usually cheerful man by the name of Thomas O'Keeffe— stared at her over his bifocals, looking just as uncertain as the people she had passed on the street.

"Mrs. Hovey, can I help you?"

His tone was fast, and his eyes were darting all around, watching everyone except Hannah.

"Yes, the cold weather has my hands in a struggle. The pain is acting up again. The rheumatism. I could barely even get a fire started."

"Ah yes," he said, leaning down and rummaging around under the counter. "Captain had me keep some of your tonic on hand just in case. It tends to take awhile to get here, so he always made sure to order it early. He was a good man, as I'm sure you well know."

"Yes, of course, and—"

O'Keeffe placed a small brown bottle on the counter. It was the exact same as all the others Captain had brought her. The mere sight of it bought relief to her. Her hands even tingled in response.

"You know the dosages, yes?"

"Yes, sir. What do I owe you?"

"Not a thing," O'Keeffe said quickly. "Captain paid for this in advance." He looked her straight in the eyes with an almost defiant gaze and repeated: "He was a good man."

She knew what he was insinuating. She knew what they all thought. But what they did not know was that Captain was not as good as everyone assumed. Hannah took it with stride. She took it all and buried it with the rest of the secrets she knew about this town and the people in it, including Captain.

She eyed the bottle for a moment, picked it up, and pocketed it. She turned away with a quick "goodbye" and headed for the door. She paused for a moment, not at all surprised that every eye was on her now. She felt it. Eight people in all, staring little daggers into her until she smiled at all of them. It seemed their throats closed so quickly that Hannah only heard a few gasps escape as she left the store and stepped back onto the porch. She noticed the old man had left his perch. She felt the cool air fill her lungs as she took in a deep breath and relaxed for a moment before she began her walk back home. Home is where she wanted to be. That's where she felt safe and where she didn't have to hear what she always heard from the people in Trumbull. And later she could sleep, because in her sleep she never had to hear what she was hearing someone screaming somewhere in the distance. "There's Hannah Cranna, the witch, the witch, the goddamn witch."

CHAPTER 7

When she returned home, the cabin was warm from the fire she had built that morning. She'd had a most precarious day but was happy to see the fire was still sputtering along just fine. She hung up her cloak and walked to the hearth room to stir the coals and shift the burning wood, figuring there might be another few hours of heat to come from it. She looked around the cabin and felt a sense of loneliness come over her. Something inside of her seized up, as if her throat were constricting and her heart were being bound by leather straps. It was the first time she truly felt alone. "Help me," she whispered as she went to the window and gazed at the forest in front of her cabin. She thought of Captain and images began to dance in her mind when they'd first met. How happy he was. How happy she was. She couldn't remember when things went so bad. But in that moment, she realized bad was better than what she had right now. It was something she had never thought of before. Then the images sprang into her mind, the vision of the man standing and watching her in the barn. Pushing it away, she then wondered when the boy would come with her wood—or if the man with the cart had been misleading her the entire time.

She decided to spend a bit of time sweeping the cabin, not because it needed it, but because she had nothing else to do. Hannah took the weed broom Captain had made her last summer and gave the cabin a quick sweep. She found that the cabin tended to stay cleaner now that Captain wasn't around. No more grime and dirt from his boots when he came in from his hunt, or pieces of the dirty dishes he broke against the wall in his drunken stupors. There was less trash to pick up and less laundry to clean. It was the one thing she had not expected about losing him—this sudden surplus of extra time and a cleaner house. Though truth be told, she would much rather have a disgusting cabin than a dead husband. She hadn't known it would turn out like this. A spectacle.

After the sweeping, she moved to the washroom. She had decided to give the tin a good scrubbing and replace her bran meal that she used when her skin felt oily. Her hands trembled as she scrubbed, but she could not remove the dried blood and scratches etched deep into the bottom of the tin.

It reminded her of the claw marks she sometimes saw in the oak trees while she strolled through the woods. But this was no oak tree, and the scratches, they were just old memories of Captain's belt buckle failing toward Hannah on nights when he was bored. She took a deep breath and thought of the matching scratches she wore across her back, then closed her eyes and tried scrubbing again.

She couldn't remember if the marks had always been etched so deep within the basin. Captain would have surely been more careful. Maybe they'd always been like that, she just didn't know. But the dirt and grime thrown about the tin, she knew it hadn't always been there, and she wondered curiously where it had come from. Frustrated, she walked back into the kitchen. A light, clattering noise filled the room. She thought the sound was coming from the front yard. She went to the window and looked out. There was a boy of about fourteen or so, carefully leading a horse into her yard. The horse was pulling a small wagon stacked high with wood. The man in town had told her it would all be scrap wood. *Boy, he wasn't kidding,* she thought. The wood was twisted and partially rotten, worse than the pieces she had used to make the fire last night. It looked to have come from old, pulverized tree stumps, likely yanked from the ground at the edge of Trumbull where more and more settlers were starting to buy land and build homes.

Hannah grabbed the thin white shawl Captain had bought her from a seamstress in Virginia on his trip out there two summers ago. She stepped out onto the porch to greet the boy. There was a slight breath of wind breaking in from the top of the pines, and Hannah tightened her grip around her forearms. The smell in the air reminded her of something that was rotting and fresh at the same time. She noticed the boy's eyes fall on her as he halted the horse. There was a strange mixture of wonder and horror in his expression as he did his best to speak, trying to put on a tone that was far more mature than his young body could muster.

"Where you want it?"

"Around back," she said. "You'll see where the last pile was. Here, I'll show you."

Hannah stepped down to lead him around to the barn, but he spoke up at once.

"That's OK," he said quickly. "I'll get it. Can you just put my money on the porch?"

Hannah paused for a moment and stared at him. She felt the same rush of sadness she'd felt earlier in the cabin.

The boy guided the horse around the side yard to the back. Hannah stood on the porch and watched him pass around, taking another look at the wood. She could not complain because the wood itself was free; she was only paying the boy for the delivery. But she knew she was being given the sort of wood that would be tossed in a cinder pile when a new plot of land was cleared. She also noticed that each piece of wood seemed very small compared to the wood from the shed last night. That meant it would not require any splitting. That was a small mercy in and of itself.

The sound of the horse's shoes pounding the ground as it went toward the barn reminded Hannah of Captain. Again, she felt the longing for his companionship. She took another swift look toward the forest, then left what she thought was an appropriate payment on the porch directly by the stairs as the boy asked. She went back inside and stood by the small window between the kitchen and bedroom, watching the boy stack the wood as well as he could. He did not stack it in any sort of organized manner, and most of it ended up looking like a messy pile, but she didn't care. It was only for burning, after all.

As the boy finished, Hannah spotted something moving in the forest at the edge of her yard near the barn. She prayed it was not any of the town boys coming back to piddle on her grass or the mysterious images from last night. She hoped it was the occasional deer that wandered out, or maybe squirrels running around at play. She had even seen a bear on one occasion. But it was neither of those things. This time it was a black rooster strutting its way out of the trees and onto the edge of her yard. A smile came over her lips, a smile so intrigued it made her shiver. She had no clear idea why, but she found the bird fascinating. It was black in color. His comb, beak, feathers, and even the wattle hanging from its chin, all as dark as night. She eyed it closely. It even seemed to cock its head at the boy inquisitively as he worked. On one occasion, Hannah watched as the rooster turned its head to look at her, spying through the window, and it reached deep inside of her, squeezing her soul.

Hannah was sure she had never seen the rooster before. She remembered Captain complaining about the Nichols' chickens on occasion, and even their cows—Captain despised the thought of the upkeep on farm animals, he always told her the animals were meant to be hunted, not fed. But Hannah had never heard him speak of a black rooster. She wasn't even sure if a solid black rooster had ever existed. Had they?

Slowly, the rooster approached the boy. When it was close enough for the boy to notice, he gave it a swift kick and the rooster barely dodged it, flapping its wings and cawing loudly as it ran away. It stopped at the edge of the yard and turned back to the boy as he tossed the last of the wood onto the raggedy pile.

Hannah noticed the rooster regarding every move the boy made. Even when the boy climbed back up behind the reins of the horse and directed him back around the house, the rooster followed with an empty gaze. Hannah felt a sensation of curiosity and could not take her eyes off the small creature. Suddenly a jangling sound on the porch broke her trance. It was the boy, collecting his payment. When Hannah turned back to look at the forest line again, she searched and searched, but the rooster was gone.

CHAPTER 8

Hannah awoke to fresh agony in her hands. She had taken her medicine shortly after her dinner of cornbread and gravy, but its effects had apparently worn off. She lay there for a moment in the darkness. The oil lamp she normally burned at night had run dry, and there was barely any light peeking in through the kitchen window. She figured it was sometime after midnight. Usually when there was sufficient light radiating through the window to see most of the room in the milky glow of the moon, Hannah knew it was somewhere near daybreak. But as she laid there staring through the cabin, she knew it was a place of darkness.

Hannah held her hands tightly to her chest, she got out of bed and stumbled, still half-asleep. Her white night dress was so thin, it did nothing to stop the sudden chill of the cabin. But the pain in her hands was so excruciating that she barely noticed.

She quickly walked to the kitchen table to fetch the tonic she'd left there before bed. But as she moved through the frigid darkness, an eerie feeling came over her. Being alone and being *aware* of that loneliness while the sun was hiding behind the clouds was bad enough, but dealing with such an empty feeling, the agony in her hands, and a dark, cold cabin was a new kind of creature.

She sat at the table, uncapped her medicine, and drank from it. As the thick liquid slid down her throat, it reminded her of the tree sap and turpentine her mother would mix when she was a child. The smell was nauseating. Once she had chased it with whiskey, but Captain always told her that ladies never do such things, so she avoided such measures at all costs.

Then there was another smell. Wood rot and pine. It blew through the cabin like a locomotive. It was another one of those special recipes from her mother, but this one was different. This one Hannah was made to drink if her mother felt Hannah was becoming well—a little unconventional. The sound of her mother's voice ricocheted through her mind. Still wincing from the pain in her hands, she felt as if she were trapped in a living nightmare. Almost desperately, she took another swig of her tonic.

Little girls that act that way turn out to be whores, her mother had told her at the age of eight. *Are you a whore, Hannah? Let me see the hand you touched yourself with. Give me your hand, Hannah.*

Usually, the memory would fade before the hammer came down. But on those rare occasions when the sound of the hammer pierced her mind, there was no stopping it. On particularly bad days, it could be as loud as summer thunder. Afterward, the trauma of it would not leave her, remaining by her side like an old friend who never knew when to leave.

With the medicine down, Hannah checked the fire. She added one sad, twisted little scrap of wood to it and stoked the coals. Even lifting the poker brought on a surge of pain, but she ignored it, praying for the medicine to do its work quickly. When she was done, she set the poker down, slammed the stove door shut and headed back to bed. The expanse of darkness between the stove and her bed looked like an ocean for a moment, and she did not want to walk into it. Nameless things lurked there, things born of the cold and her pain, things that would soak into her and present themselves in the form of nightmares. Still, wanting the warmth of the blankets and the relative comfort of sleep, she walked quickly toward it.

She took two steps before a scream began to rise in her throat.

Something was curled in the center of the floor, between the stove and the door to her bedroom. Even in the dark, she was quite sure it was something black. It made her think of the rooster from earlier in the day as it strutted back and forth on the line of her property, surveying it and studying it. But this was no rooster. As it coiled its body closer to her, she knew what it was. A snake. A black snake. She knew that black snakes were good to have around a homeplace. They killed rodents and kept small critters from ruining vegetable gardens. They were said to be a nuisance for anyone keeping chickens, though, as they liked to feast on eggs.

She waited, watching it and smiling a little to herself when she thought about the Good Book and how Christians were always talking about how the serpent was responsible for the fall of man. It seemed like a fitting little story for the evil-looking creatures. Once she'd watched one swallow a feral kitten whole, and it had been one of the most exciting things she had ever witnessed.

Hannah thought the best thing to do now was to grab a broom from the corner of the kitchen and carefully walk around the snake. The darkness did not seem like a threat anymore; now all she knew was the snake, as if the darkness had manifested it somehow. Hannah kept her back to the wall, pressing against it to stay as far away from the serpent as she could. She felt like a silly, scared teenage girl that was about to lose her flower. She pushed at it with the bristle end of her broom. The snake curled up a bit but looked to be just as tired and out of sorts as Hannah had been upon waking.

She scooted the creature to the door, and it did not complain. Wondering how the damned thing had gotten into the cabin in the first place, she opened the door. The final shove she gave to the snake was rather harsh, and it was sent tumbling over itself off the porch and thudding down the stairs.

"Serves you right," she said under her breath.

She grabbed the door to close it, perhaps with a triumphant shove, but stopped. There was something there on her porch, something hunkered down in the dark. It was small, but alive. It was the rooster.

"What are you doing here?" Hannah asked it. "Don't you have a home?"

The bit of mischief fell over her, she felt connected to the small bird. It seemed pleasant in a peculiar way. Oddly enough, it was the first real form of joy she had felt since Captain died. She felt a strange innocence and sense of wonder that she had not felt in a very long time.

"Get on out of here," she said to the rooster. "Shoo."

The rooster barely moved in the darkness. His eyes glowed like stars, and as Hannah closed the door behind her, the whispers began, pushing through like a gust of stale wind. She heard the rooster respond to her, only with a voice from her past.

Let me see the hand you touched yourself with. Give me your hand, Hannah. Give it to me! Are you a whore Hannah?

CHAPTER 9

A carriage came down the trail the following morning. It was rather early. Hannah had just finished a breakfast of buttered bread and oats. She had a yearning for eggs but was nearly out, so she decided to save them. Plus, she wasn't quite ready for another trip into town. Apparently, though, town was coming to her. She opened her door and felt a cool rush of air as she watched a carriage come to a stop in front of her cabin. The early hour made her wonder if the visitor was concerned about being seen with her. Maybe the townspeople were stirring up more gossip and mayhem. "Wouldn't want to be seen with the witch," Hannah whispered as she grabbed her cloak off the peg and stepped out onto the porch.

As the horses came to a halt, Hannah peered toward the

carriage and noticed a middle-aged man with a long beard that was a healthy mix of black and gray. He was wearing a well-tailored suit and the sort of hat that reminded her of President Lincoln. When he started across the yard and saw Hannah looking at him, he took his hat off and gave her a polite little bow.

"Kinda early for a visit, isn't it, sir?" Hannah said, wrapping her cloak tighter around her arms.

"G'morning, Mrs. Hovey," the man said. "My name is Alexander Hoffman, and I am sorry for the time. I am a loan officer and partner at Trumbull Bank. I was wondering if I might have a word with you about your late husband's final affairs."

Hannah cocked her head toward him, her long braid shifting on her shoulders. She eyed him cautiously and hesitated, recalling the last time a man had visited her cabin. That had been Pastor Dunne. The awkwardness and tension of that visit still seemed to hang in the air, but as selfish as it made her seem, she figured this was a meeting she *needed* to have. Like it or not, she was going to have to rely on whatever money Captain had left her. She assumed it would be a pretty penny since he had always been financially responsible.

"Fine," she finally said, stepping aside to allow him entrance. He paused the moment he came into the door, looking around skeptically.

"Something wrong, Mr. Hoffman?"

"No-no, ma'am," he said, though she knew he was lying. She found herself looking at the floor, smiling. She thought of the snake from last night and glanced around again, making sure there were no other unexpected visitors on her floor. It made her wonder what type of witch stories would circulate around town if this banker went back claiming that she lived with snakes. A slight titter escaped, but Hannah drew it back in as she walked to the table in the kitchen and took a seat. She nodded at one of the two free chairs, and the man joined her at the table.

"I do apologize for the nature of this visit," Mr. Hoffman said. "I personally feel rather vile whenever I have to speak about the finances of the dead. But the law, being as it is, requires that I do so. Are you OK to have this conversation?"

"Yes, of course. I mean, yes, I understand." Hannah shuffled nervously in her chair. She wasn't sure if it was the unfamiliarity of having a man sitting in Captain's chair or the effort of trying not to seem so eager to find out about Captain's money. She just hoped the old banker didn't notice.

"Very well," Mr. Hoffman said. He stared peculiarly at Hannah. She could feel his cold gaze as he reached into the inner pocket of his suit jacket and pulled out a piece of paper that had been folded three times vertically. He unfolded it and lay it on the table, revealing that it was two sheets of paper. On the bottom of the second, Hannah saw Captain's signature scrawled across a line. The sight of it made her profoundly sad, but she wasn't sure why.

"This," Hoffman said, "is your husband's last will and testament. It makes it quite clear where he wanted his property and finances to go if he passed away. Now, there is verbiage in here that makes it known that the will, as it stands, was liable to be changed by Mr. Hovey at any time he saw fit, and whenever such a clause is added, there's usually a good chance that the individual does indeed plan to change it in due time. However, seeing that he can no longer make changes to it, the law requires that we keep the wishes as they are written in the will at present. Do you understand?"

"Yeah, can we just move along?" Hannah said, fiddling with her fingers and then confirmed it with a nod, though she didn't understand why he was using language that was clearly intended to confuse her. She also wondered why the banker seemed to be going out of his way to stress this point.

"OK then," Hoffman said. "By accordance of this last will and testament of Lawrence Hovey, exactly eighty percent of his savings and other accrued monies will be transferred to James Hovey, Lawrence's brother."

Hannah felt as if someone had stabbed her in the chest and given the blade a sudden turn. She had only met James once, and that was immediately after the wedding. A pompous and arrogant son of a bitch if she'd ever met one. It had been quite clear to her that James despised his brother.

He thought Captain was living on the side of the devil, marrying Hannah. But based on the few instances where Captain had mentioned James, the hostility was mutual. It made absolutely no sense that Captain would...

"You seem confused," Hoffman said.

"They just...well, Captain and James did not care for one another."

"That's the rumor I hear as well. Although, I hear it is because of you, Mrs. Hovey. But I guess that don't matter none, does it?"

"I guess it doesn't," Hannah lashed back.

"I'll tell you that with my job, I see this all the time. Usually with sons and fathers, but occasionally with siblings as well. One will often leave money to their surviving estranged relatives as a form of forgiveness or reconciliation—mending burned bridges after they have died. A way to forgive without any actual interaction." He gave her a moment to collect her thoughts.

"The remaining twenty percent, as well as the cabin in which we currently sit and the land it occupies, were left for you, with a stipulation of course."

"Stipulation? What stipulation?"

"Well, Mrs. Hovey, you are a woman. You are not allowed to own property. So, Mr. Hovey, concerned about you, set up a stipulation. You were to remain in the cabin without no burden until you join him in the afterlife."

"So, what's the stipulation?" Hannah demanded. "Say it!"

"Well...then the cabin and all this land goes to...the church, Mrs. Hovey."

"Goddamn thievery!"

"Mrs. Hovey, you must understand..."

"This is my home! Not those goddamn bastards of that godless church! They will never get my home. Their all lying pigs. They can't steal my land."

Hannah watched as Mr. Hoffman's eyes widened. He leaned back in his chair. "That's blasphemy, Mrs. Hovey. Pure blasphemy. And it's church law."

"To hell with you and this town! To hell with that damn church and its law! What else?" Hannah said, her voice cracked as she lowered her head. "What else, sir?" Countless emotions tore through her like tiny hooks in her muscles, shredding and tearing. *Give me your hands, Hannah* whispered through the cabin as the door burst open. A gust of wind blew the pages of the will off the table, and they fluttered across the floor. Hannah smiled. Mr. Hoffman nervously pushed his chair back and retrieved the papers. Hannah scurried toward the door and looked out across her yard. Standing in the distance, the black rooster stood stoically, staring, guarding. Hannah stared back defiantly and then shut the door.

As she walked back toward the table, she looked back at the door and thought about the rooster. Then she looked at

Mr. Hoffman. His hands were shaking slightly as Hannah went around the table and sat back down.

"Is there anything else?"

"This is the statement for your twenty percent," Hoffman said, pulling another paper from his jacket like some sort of wizard. "It was drafted just this morning, along with one for James. James, of course, lives down in Virginia, so that will be handled via telegram. This, though, is currently in an account for you down at the bank. I believe everything has cleared and is in order. You'll just need to sign a few papers."

Hannah looked at the statement and felt a little wash of shame. She had been so angry that her husband, the man who supposedly loved her yet treated her like a dirty swine at times, had only left her twenty percent. But looking at the figures on the statement, it was much more than she had expected. This twenty percent of Captain's savings and earnings would sustain her for about a year and a half, and she would live comfortably for that time, so long as the people of Trumbull did not make things unnecessarily difficult.

"Do you have any questions?" Hoffman asked.

But still, she thought. *Imagine what that piss ant James is going to do with the eighty percent. Whiskey, whores, and land he'll never use, no doubt.*

"No," she said bitterly. "Now get out of *my* cabin."

As Hoffman nodded and collected his papers, she saw that he was again looking around the place as if he didn't trust it. When he stood up, he did so quickly, the professionalism and manners he had shown so far were all gone now.

"Well, if you have any questions at a later date," Hoffman said, "I'll be happy to help."

"I said get out!"

"Good day, Mrs. Hovey."

"Piss off!" Hannah said.

She watched him step out onto the porch. She smiled about what she had already seen there, coiled and waiting. As Hoffman took a second step, Hannah's eyes locked on the shape less than six inches away from the banker's left foot.

Hoffman took another step and nearly landed on the serpent. He corrected his course with a spastic little jump, letting out a yelp of surprise and nearly falling off the porch. He looked at Hannah in shock, and she smiled fiendishly. For the briefest flicker of time, he had thought she intended for this to happen—that she had somehow orchestrated it.

"Lord Jesus, you are a devilish woman!" he yelled as he finally reached the stairs.

The snake slithered just a bit in response but was ultimately unhindered by the commotion. Hannah said nothing to Hoffman, just watched him go as a smile stretched across on her face. When the carriage was turned and headed back to town, Hannah turned her attention to the snake. She took a step closer to it, picked it up, and allowed it to slither and coil around her arm. She grinned at its shape, appreciating it, and praising it.

CHAPTER 10

The cold settled in that night, thick and vicious. Before retiring to bed, Hannah stacked the stove the best she could. She quickly realized that the scrap and rejected pieces of wood were a stinker to set alight, but once they *did* catch, they burned for quite a while. With only the slightest of aches in her hands, she settled down and found sleep comfortably.

She dreamed of Captain, as she had a few times since his death, but this dream was more of a recollection infected by the silly fantasies of dreams. She dreamed of their wedding night and the day after. Captain had asked if they could spend their wedding night in the woods, next to a waterfall he had frequented for fishing and swimming as a boy. She had agreed with enthusiasm, as she had always felt a strange yet beautiful connection to nature.

They remained in the woods for two days and three nights. She lost count of how many times they made love; she had received it both gently and soul-piercing, as well as harsh and borderline violent—and she loved it all. On that final night, as the moon was high in the sky and pulling in the early morning hours, they went swimming in the small pool beneath the waterfall. Coming out of it, they made love on a large, water-worn rock just at the edge of the pool.

Even now, seven years later and in a dream-state, Hannah remembered it vividly. Something about the rock pressing hard against her back, scratching at her skin, the moon glaring down, the waterfall churning, and the pool reflecting the sky caused her to climax ridiculously fast. The handful of minutes that followed had been something resembling ecstasy. For a moment she heard the stars singing, the waterfall humming in tune, and the world— every single bit of it—was connected. It all sang to her, praising them as one flesh, promising her a grand life of preservation.

Only, in her dream, when Captain was finished and kissed her neck with exhausted breaths, he bit down on her flesh. It was arousing at first, but then she felt her veins pulsating as the warm blood dripped down her breast. For a moment even *that* was pleasurable, but then the whispers came. And when she writhed beneath him, the dream taking a firm hold, the soft voice inside her head seemed to come from an angel, but everything inside of her went cold at the words he spoke.

"There are no devils..."

She awoke with a shriek, sitting up in bed, realizing that at some point in the dream—perhaps the more realistic and erotic parts—she had managed to remove her sleeping garments as she dozed. She panted for breath as that last comment echoed in her sleepy mind: *There are no devils... there are no devils...there are no—*

Beads of sweat collected on her temples as a slight whisper bounced off the walls, sending chills dancing on her skin. A bit of panic stuck in her throat and remained there. A black void dug into her like an old friend. There was something there in the darkness, standing in the corner like evil, just passing through. Then came a noise from outside the cabin. It was a sudden *thunk*, followed by a light clatter. It came again, and then a third time. Hannah's eyes widened and remained staring, watching the figure that stood watching her. Then it morphed into nothing but dust and disappeared, the same way it had that night near the barn. Hannah slowly slid into her bedclothes. The thin fabric absorbed the sweet drops of her sweat like a sponge. She slowly got up and walked to the window, already fairly certain of what she would see.

Sure enough, there were two boys outside holding an old oil lantern, pointing it toward her cabin. They stood right at the edge of her yard, looking like little rogue ghosts in the waning moonlight. The forest behind them resembled a dark stitchwork of random shapes, harsh and jagged against the night.

Had it not been for the nightmare, Hannah may have just let them go on and have their fun. So long as they stayed out of her yard and posed no real threat, she honestly did not see the harm. But the nightmare had her on edge. She walked to the front door and opened it slowly, hoping it would make enough noise to startle the boys and they would run away.

She could just barely hear them from the porch. It seemed that one of them was whispering. She heard rustling leaves, maybe the other was looking around the edge of the yard, presumably looking for another rock. That boy froze when he looked in her direction. She guessed them to be quite young—no older than twelve or thirteen.

Hannah stepped out onto the porch with her arms crossed over her chest. It was damn cold, but it was a relief from the heat she had felt minutes ago when something tore her from her sleep.

"Scat, you scathed rats! What are you boys doing out there? I see you out there!" Hannah yelled, trying to adjust her eyes with the reflection of the lantern against the darkened sky.

One of the boys started snickering nervously as the

other started backing away. She heard another little whisper between them, and the rock-thrower summoned up one last bit of bravery.

"Nothing, you ol' witch!"

Hannah watched as they turned and started to run, but after a few steps, the smaller boy's ankle gave way, and he stumbled and fell forward. Something in the forest moved quickly, a flutter of darkness among the paler spaces between the trees. Hannah thought of the presence she had sensed by the barn that night and again moments ago in her bedroom—something slinking quietly in the shadows. Something that *thrived* in the darkness and took up its residence there.

But this was different. And as the little boy started to shout, Hannah saw a dark image land on his back, clawing at his skin. As she watched, smiling, she heard a strange noise coming from that shifting darkness. It was a soft beating, the fluttering of busy wings. A clucking sort of cry echoed through the forest, not a protest, but an almost joyful noise. Her legs trembled but she pressed forward and took another step, eventually to the edge of the porch. Hannah stretched her eyes through the gloom and saw the image that was attacking the boy.

It was the black rooster. It was out there, just beyond the grips of darkness. It was fluttering in the smaller boy's face now and pecking at his skin, tearing at his eyes. The boy was wailing and slapping out blindly, striking nothing as the larger boy grabbed him by the arm, fought off the rooster, and quickly hauled the child away. Wild screams tore through the forest as the rooster gave chase for a moment and then stopped. Hannah remained on her porch, watching the rooster strut with pride, and stared eagerly at the road.

She slowly walked down the steps, never taking her keen eye off the black creature that protected her. She watched as he strutted in victory, fluttering his wings, black as midnight, sparkling elegance like a million stars in the darkened sky. He strutted to the center of the road, cocked his head toward her and stopped. He allowed her to see every definition of him even in the darkness of night. And he was triumphant.

She had no idea why, but the comment from her nightmare echoed in her head as the sound of the fleeing boys grew fainter and fainter.

There are no devils.

CHAPTER 11

Hannah woke reluctantly, she presumed from the cold that had inched into her bones over the past four nights. There were no more nightmares and no more children, and she was thankful for that. But the rooster still showed up from time to time. One afternoon she found it sitting on her porch, peering out toward the road as if it were expecting company. A ring of dead insects and perfectly halved worms, dried and brittle, laid at his feet in a full circle. But often, she would catch it walking back and forth across the edge of her yard, specifically to the road. He looked like a little knight from the tales her father had told her before he had died—tales about dragons, knights, queens, and princesses, all in some faraway land. Her little black knight seemed to be quite interested in her property, and that was fine with her. Maybe he could keep those troublesome critters away, and maybe even a Trumbull dragon or two.

After she finished her cold oats, she brought in a few pieces of firewood. She noticed that she only had a few lengths left—maybe enough for three days, it was hard to accurately judge with these knotted, rejected pieces. Hannah spied the day. It was considerably warmer than the last few, and she figured she could make the walk back into town. So she dressed in her widow's weeds. Some referred to it as a mourning dress. She thought maybe she could conjure up some sympathy from the men in Trumbull if she reminded them, she was just a widow. She felt a little ball develop in her stomach. *Nerves*, she thought. She hoped her hands would not respond to the chill in the air, though they tended to behave when the sun was high in the sky, no matter how biting the cold might be.

She walked down Crow Trail, noticing as she left the yard that the black rooster was still strutting around on the edge of the woods. At the time, he was happily pecking at something among the fallen leaves.

She passed by the houses along her road, keeping her head down. She knew it was silly, but the visit from the two boys had troubled her more than she cared to admit. Calling her a witch had not upset her, but the daring little way they had stood at the edge of her yard burdened her more and more every time she thought about it. She was also bothered by the way the rooster attacked them. She was not prepared for the scolding those little bastards had conjured up. In Trumbull, she was sure the gossip was that now the witch can control roosters. That, she was not prepared for.

She passed by only a single person—an elderly woman walking with a crooked cane—on her way into the town proper. She was rather ashamed that she had lost track of the days over the past two weeks or so. Sitting around the cabin and doing next to nothing tended to drain the importance out of life. She had no idea if it was Monday or Sunday, but whatever day it was, it was a slow one in Trumbull.

The town was nothing more than a scattered collection of wooden buildings along a flat stretch of usually muddy ground. Old Crow Trail led directly into it. The town absorbed the road, which ran on for about a quarter of a mile. It boasted poor, struggling businesses, and then dipped down the track a bit, leading out into the woods. Another plot was being cleared by woodsmen on the other side of town—presumably for more homes and businesses. Rumor had it that some people from down South were starting to trickle up North, and it was evident in seemingly mundane projects like these.

As for Trumbull, it was almost always slow during the week. Today was more of the same. There was hardly anyone out on the streets. Even the stoop of the general store and saloon was vacant. Hannah guessed it really must be Monday and sensed something was happening. Also empty was the small square of space between buildings where the lumber cart had been the last time she had come to town. She expected the same sort of deal she had received last time, and if it had to be those wretched scraps of wood, well, she would just have to make do. But without him here, she had no idea where to look. It was another way in which she had relied far too much on Captain. He had literally taken care of everything, careful to make sure they were always comfortable. Hannah needed to go by the grocer's as well, so she supposed she could ask him where to look for wood.

"You lookin' for Douglas?"

Hannah turned at the sound of this voice. There was a man standing by the general store, leaning cautiously against the wooden structure, twirling a hay straw between his teeth. He was a younger man, maybe in his early twenties. Clean-shaven and with crystal blue eyes, he stood out a bit more than the other men of Trumbull. He regarded Hannah with a curious expression, but she much preferred this look over the caution and fear she had been getting from everyone else in town.

"Douglas?" Hannah said, walking closer to the man.

"Yeah, Douglas, the man that delivered you wood."

"I don't know his name."

"Yeah, that's Douglas. Sorry, he's done for a bit." The

man said, pushing himself off the building, walking closer to Hannah. "Might be awhile. His wife fell like a sap, after childbirth. Ain't lookin good."

"Oh, I see."

"But maybe I can help you. I mean, if it's firewood you're needing, and all."

"Is that right?"

"It is. I don't do it as a job like Douglas, but I have an ax, and there are trees all around, right? I'd ask to be paid, of course."

"Of course," she said, as she stared at the man incredulously. "How soon can you get it out to my land?"

"I'd say tomorrow, about the same time."

"And the price?" she asked, raising her brow, darting her eyes toward him.

"I'm sure we can work something out," he said, smiling. He ran his tongue across his teeth. "Why don't we start by heading over to one of the rooms at the inn? If you're as full of evil as some people around here think you are, I imagine you'd be like fire in the bedroom." He leaned in, so close their noses were almost touching. "But I'd want it from behind, you know. I can't bugger a widow if I can see her eyes."

Hannah turned her back and hurried away from him. The ice of shame and the roaring fire of rage stirred inside of her and came out as a neutral defeat. As she walked quickly toward the grocer's, she could hear the man cackling behind her. "You *do* look good from the backside! I never screwed a witch before."

She felt anger and embarrassment, as well as that same old fire and ice, dueling inside of her. It was a battle that lasted until she reached the grocer's shop. When she walked in, a single tear had made its way down her cheek, but she swatted it away quickly. She badly wanted to be back at her cabin, away from this wretched town and its vile people. Without paying much attention to her surroundings, Hannah made her way around the grocer's aisles and selected the things she needed— a bag of corn meal, a can of lard, some dry beans, and butter. She needed eggs too, but she would have to get those from one of the local farmer vendors—a task she didn't even want to think about as she weaved her way through the grocer's store.

She approached the grocer with her items in hand. An elderly man was at the counter with a young girl wearing a gray dress with pigtails draped in a white bow. Hannah provoked a smile from her as she was selecting a lollipop from one of the grocer's glass containers. The two men seemed to notice Hannah at the same time. The elderly stepped in, Hannah presumed it was the girl's father, he stepped closer, pulling her securely to his side. The girl smiled again at Hannah, and the man quickly paid for the two lollipops the little girl had been debating over. The grocer thanked them, and when the man left, he turned back to Hannah, searching her face. Hannah stepped forward and placed her items on the counter.

The grocer was a middle-aged man who, as far as Hannah knew, had always been friendly with Captain. Now he regarded her with weary eyes, his mouth creating a solid, thin line that broke his bushy, ill-kept beard.

"Good of ya to stop in, Mrs. Hovey," he said.

"Of course. I know Captain spoke hi—"

"If you're gonna keep coming here for your groceries, I'll need you to send a list and pick it up out back. I can't have ya coming in here anymore."

Again, Hannah felt that flicker of anger rising up inside of her. She leaned forward, pushing back any urge to cry, and felt it burn like hot iron in her chest. "And why might that be?"

The grocer took a step back. "Well, Mrs. Hovey this is a Christian town. People are talking, and I can't have you coming in here or people'll be thinking my store is cursed."

"Well, that's just foolish. These people are lying pigs! Some Christians you speak of!"

"Maybe so," he said, starting to calculate her purchases. "But from here on out, that's just the way it's going to have to be. Now, if you'd like, I can also work with Bruce Hamlet, the farmer I sometimes tag along with to get corn and potatoes in here. We'll make sure you don't go hungry, but that's the best I can do, considering your reputation.

And of course, I would have to charge a fee for my services of helping you and all."

"A fee? Of course. Wouldn't that be going against church law? I mean, doing business with a witch and all?"

He nodded and looked away, his cheeks growing red at the sides of his beard. He bagged up her goods and recited her price: "Ninety cents."

"Do you know how these rumors came to be?" she asked.

Hannah watched him closely. Her eyes went dark as he finally answered.

"Depends on who you ask. The way I hear it, you bewitched and ensnared a much-loved Christian man in Captain Hovey. Some say you had a hand in his death. But let Captain Hovey rest because his major loss was the loss of his good name when he married you. You are not womanly. Your sharp tongue speaks of evil against sensibilities of the great people of Trumbull."

"Great people?" she said, "I am a mourning widow, and you have all abandoned any notion of helping me like your Good Book says. And the tongue words that are slung out the mouth of the pastor on Sunday mornings! It's like a punishment for the death of my husband."

"Not a punishment, Mrs. Hovey. The good Christian people of this proper town cannot be drawn into the darkness, not the darkness you possess. It is all around you. Remember, God forgives all."

"Oh, I see...so when the pastor speaks of love and sympathy for widows and the town rejects me, that is acceptable to your God? It's fine, Mr. Mean. But you all just wait...wait until you see my punishment. You damn harlots!

"Mrs. Hovey, there is no need for blasphemy or threats. God loves us all," he said, as if it freed him of any guilt.

Hannah let out a loud laugh, almost braying, and it seemed to scare the grocer. She leaned in and whispered, "I don't need your God to love me." The grocer looked away again and pushed the sack of groceries over to her. Then, without another word, he walked away from the counter and gave his attention to the back storage shelves.

As she made her way to the door, angry furrows in her mind were suddenly replaced with something else. She could not put a name to it, but it felt like acceptance. As a smile developed across her lips, something deep down coiled inside of her. *There are no devils,* she thought as she walked out the door.

CHAPTER 12

On the way back to the cabin, carrying her sack of groceries cradled against her chest, Hannah played over in her mind the conversation she had with the grocer. She wondered if she'd been too brazen with him, maybe given the town more to hold against her. But Hannah knew she was not always like that. She was usually kind and accepting of others. But then she'd married Captain and endured his cruel and sometimes uncaring ways. Now he was dead, and she was left to fend for herself, and the whole experience had changed her. Already a hard-working woman, tending to her dead husband's wishes, caring for her home, trying to fit in a town that did not like outsiders, Hannah was handling it as well as she could. Maybe that was the cause of her so benevolent nature. And maybe that is why part of her wanted to turn around, walk back into Trumbull, and thank the grocer for the help he did offer. But what would that do?

Something tore Hannah out of her thoughts. It was the robust smell of sausages and smells that were sweet and indicative, almost nostalgic, coming from Elmer Jefferson's place. Then she heard children laughing in the distance. It was coming from up ahead. She glanced through the stripped trees and saw that the joyous sounds were coming from the Nichols's' barren yard. Their two girls were playing. One was but a toddler—the one Hannah had spotted chasing a squirrel with a stick several days ago—and the other looked to be about ten or so. The older one looked very much like her mother, Emma Nichols, and carried herself with both grace and strength even at such a young age. She carried her chin and nose up in a way that suggested she might be a spitfire when she got older.

Hannah smiled in their direction, but neither girl noticed her as they played some strange form of tag with what looked to be a chicken's feather. Just before she passed the house, Hannah saw and smelled something. The front door was open despite the cold, and Hannah caught a whiff of fresh-baked apple pie. It was one of those smells that was unmistakable. Hannah had not had an apple pie in quite a while—since Captain had died. It had always been a special treat, a way to redeem his barbaric behavior. Standing in front of the Nichols property and smelling the special treat she wondered if Captain had purchased the pie from Emma Nichols. The scent was intoxicating.

Before she was fully aware of what she was doing, Hannah found herself entering the yard and walking toward the house. Within a few steps, the girls noticed her, and their laughter faded. The children grinned nervously. The older girl reached out and nudged her sister, and they both took off running back to the house. The feather they had been playing with fluttered in the air in their wake.

Hannah walked slowly toward the porch. She figured with the girls rushing inside in a giddy sort of panic she would not have to knock. She fully expected Emma or Rube Nichols to come out, so she made sure she did not step foot on their doorstep. Within seconds, Hannah saw a figure walking toward her. It was Emma Nichols. The younger girl was clinging to her leg, looking out curiously with a large smile on her face.

"What do you want, Hannah?" Emma asked with equal parts irritation and fear in her voice.

"Sorry to bother you," Hannah said. "I couldn't help but smell apple pie as I was walking by. I always heard you made the best pies in Trumbull—maybe in the entire county."

"That's kind of you to say. Can I help you with something?" It was clear she wanted Hannah gone, and the compliment hadn't done much to appeal to her kindness. Emma's hands were placed on her ample hips, and despite the bit of fear Hannah sensed coming from the woman, she stood resolute and unmoving.

"I was simply walking by and would love one of those pies. I wanted to see if I could purchase one," Hannah said, shifting her groceries to her hip.

Hannah watched as all the color left Emma's face. The dark circles under her eyes told a story of nothing but terror and exhaustion. Her pale skin took on a grayish tinge. It reminded Hannah of the grocer's face when she had told him she did not need his God. For a split second, Hannah thought she saw something like sympathy in the woman's eyes, but it was gone as quickly as it appeared.

"No. Now get on outta here, Hannah Hovey. Go on. I can't be seen with you. Now go."

Hannah felt all her emotions slide away as she watched Emma Nichols swat her away like a housefly. She felt it in her skin, her face, and deep inside, way down in her gut. She blinked away the cool harsh breeze that escaped from the forest behind her and whipped violently through her hair. She lowered her head, defeated, and turned to walk away. According to Captain, Emma Nichols was not only the best baker in Trumbull, but also an intensely God-fearing woman. Hannah knew from the woman's reaction that she had heard the rumors and had believed them. Now there was no doubt about how she felt about Hannah. It was a small mercy, Hannah thought, that the woman was even speaking with her at all.

"Thanks all the same," Hannah said, turning back to her. There was no point in arguing or adding fuel to the already foul rumors. Now the smell of the apple pie seemed to push her away just as strong as it had lured her in. She started to leave, then looked back to Emma again.

"Mrs. Nichols?"

"Yes?" the woman asked, trying to peel the toddler from her leg.

"Whatever you've heard about me, it's not true. I know what others say about me. You seem like a kind woman, and I thought maybe you could see it."

"Well," Emma said, searching for the appropriate thing to say. "That truth is between you and the Good Lord above, I suppose."

It was pretty much the response Hannah had expected, but it was still disappointing. She headed back toward the road, groceries still clutched in her arms and the smell of fresh apple pie haunting her like an eager ghost. She expected to hear the children back out in the yard now that she was gone, but the yard, and the entire stretch of Crow Trail for that matter, remained quiet.

CHAPTER 13

When Hannah returned home, she stopped several feet away from where her yard met the edge of Crow Trail. She stared into the dying grass, her legs frozen and her heart jumping like a jackrabbit in her chest. She was so shocked that she almost dropped her grocery sack.

Her yard was alive with movement. For a moment, she thought the lawn was breathing, that the earth was taking in deep, shuddering breaths and then releasing them. The ground slithered and bucked, slid and dipped right before her eyes. Finally, she realized that it was not the earth that was moving, but something *upon* it.

Snakes. So many snakes! There had to be at least a hundred of them, slithering end to end, entwining among one another. There were black snakes, copperheads, water moccasins, and little green garter snakes crawling over one another in what she could only describe as a dance.

With terror spiking her heart, Hannah took a step forward. She was not sure why, but the snakes seemed almost inviting of her lifelong acceptance of them, though that acceptance felt like nothing more than mist in that moment. As she took another step, she felt something dissolve completely, giving way to an odd sort of peace and understanding, as if something in her mind that had once been clogged was now clear.

And with that odd sensation, the snakes slithered and separated, reminding Hannah of a story in Captain's Bible, when the Red Sea parted for the Israelites. The creatures left a path in their wake for Hannah to enter.

She understood in that moment that they had accepted her. They trusted her and worshipped her. But as she passed through her yard, the snakes disappeared. She looked at the ground with distrusting eyes as they slithered back into the forest. Once again, she felt sad and alone. They'd left so quickly that she wondered if they'd been there at all. *Of course, they had*, she thought. They bowed to her, they worshipped her, but now that they'd gone, the ground was just as dead and featureless as ever. She stepped up on the porch and, just as she was heading through the cabin door, Hannah gave the yard one last glance. She found the yard empty and motionless—not a snake in sight.

Yet she understood that even if they were gone, she did not care. Her fears were gone. Her fear of everything. It was so freeing that for a moment, she could almost feel her feet levitating above the earth, sending her into a feeling of reverence for the creatures that just changed her life.

Smiling, Hannah closed the door and rested her back against it. Her eyes gazed around the floor, looking for her slithering friend from a few nights ago. She wondered if he had found his way back in somehow. Sadly, he was not there. She exhaled a long breath, walked to her table, and set her bags down, then put her groceries away. Once that was done, a chill crept into her skin, a signal she would have to head back outside to bring in the remainder of her firewood. As she opened the door, she eyed the yard carefully and walked out onto the porch, then down the steps, making sure she stayed close to the house, continuing to cast untrusting glances at the yard. Not because she feared the snakes, but because she had no idea what strange sights her brain might conjure up next.

Hannah gathered the last pieces of wood from the side of the house and walked quickly back inside. She fed the fire in the stove with a few pieces of wood. As the fire caught, she heard the searing of the flames. She turned and set the rest of the wood by the wall. A sharp pain danced across her hand,

and she moaned. She found her tonic in the cupboard and took a swig, sighing as the thick liquid slid down her throat and bottomed out in her stomach. She hoped the pain would fade quickly.

Hannah hung her cloak on the wood peg by the door and decided to sit in a chair in front of the stove as she waited for the pain in her hands to die down. As she sat, she realized that without Captain, it was certainly going to be a dull, flavorless life. She also knew that if she stayed around here, in this town full of devils, she may not survive. For the first time since Captain's death, she looked around the two-room cabin and actually considered leaving Trumbull. The silence of the house was almost deafening.

She wasn't sure how long she had been sitting there when a sound from her porch broke her concentration. It sounded like scratching, but very faint. She ignored it at first, but it came again, a bit louder this time and rather persistent. With fear sinking into her bones, she began to think about the image she'd seen in her bedroom and by the barn. She slowly got to her feet and walked to the door. Her first thought was maybe the meddlesome boys had finally gathered enough nerve to make it to her door. Then she remembered the snake. Maybe it was slithering along, trying to find a way in. But the noise was more solid than that of a slithering serpent.

Curiosity got the best of her. She reached for the knob and, as her hand fell on it, a terrifying vision filled her head.

It was there only for a moment, but it jarred her nonetheless. She saw an image of Captain standing on the other side of the door. He was dead and partially rotted away, his fleshless fingers scratching uselessly at the knob as he tried to open the door and couldn't. He was there to take her, to take her away from this town, from this world. And the most startling thing of all was Hannah's realization that she would gladly go with him. She would go with the man that was the biggest devil of all.

She blinked the image away and pulled the door open quickly. For a paralyzing moment, she fully expected to see him there. She wondered what his dead embrace would feel like, how cold his dead body would be now that it had been in the ground for a while, what he would smell like, what his cold, colorless lips would taste like.

Of course, Captain was not there.

But the rooster was. The same black rooster that had chased the two boys from the edge of her property. He looked up at her and cocked his head to the side. He then pecked gently at the doorstep—three rapid-fire consecutive pecks—and looked back up at her. It was almost as if he were paying a visit, knocking the only way he knew how and then waiting to be invited inside.

"You want to come inside?" Hannah asked, smiling. "I don't know about that. I don't think I'd enjoy cleaning rooster droppings from the floor."

He pecked at the ground once more and again looked up at her. His oddly colored eyes—somewhere between brown and red around his black pupil—seemed to study her. She recalled how he had been there to chase those meddlesome youths away and shrugged. Was he back to be repaid for his generosity and help? It seemed ridiculous at first, but there was a certain levity to it that she could not shake. Almost like a connection.

"Sure. Why not? I might enjoy the company."

She stepped back and opened the door wider. The rooster extended its neck a bit and peered inside, and after only a moment's hesitation, it strutted its way past Hannah, ruffling its feathers and staring back at her as it passed through.

Hannah left the door open a moment longer just in case the rooster changed its mind, but it was already heading for the kitchen table, exploring the floor beneath it. She could not tell if he was looking for crumbs, bugs, or some other picky factor roosters might have about how to choose their dwellings.

Not wanting to let out any of the warmth from the stove, Hannah closed the door again. When she turned back to the rooster, she was surprised at just how natural it felt to have him there. If she were being honest, it was just nice to have something moving about the cabin again aside from herself. It was a strange feeling, but one she accepted.

"I guess you can make yourself at home," she said. "But

when you feel the call of nature, you better go pecking at the door again. Are we understood?"

The rooster pecked at the floor—whether to retrieve a crumb of food or as an answer, she was not sure. As he looked at her, his curious gaze reminded her of the man who had often come into her mother's home when she was a girl. Her mother had said he was only a friend, but Hannah had always thought he was more than that. He would come for a few days, have his fill of food, drink, and her mother, and then leave for weeks at a time. He had always seemed confused and curious about things, like he never quite belonged anywhere. Hannah had not thought of him in a very long time, but his image came to her now just as clear as her own hand in front of her eyes. As the rooster looked at her, she saw her mother's friend in that inquisitive stare.

The name of the man came to her through the cobwebs and fog of her memory. She chuckled at the ease in which it came to her. "Boreas," she said. "Old Boreas. I believe that's what I'll call you."

The rooster ruffled its feathers again and made a low and pleasant noise with its throat in response. Then it continued to explore the rest of the cabin, making itself at home. It was almost as if he already knew the place quite well.

CHAPTER 14

Hannah woke up the following morning to the sight of Old Boreas perched at the end of her bed. It reminded her of the old rooster statues that churches displayed on the steeples, reminding their people how the Apostle Peter had betrayed Jesus. Hannah always figured it was another one of those old fables they used to try to get people into church, but she knew it would take more than a rusty old rooster to get her to believe in something she just couldn't get her head around.

"Yup. No church for us," Hannah said, running her fingers through her hair. Old Boreas ruffled his feathers as she slid to the edge of the bed and got up. "No way in hell." The rooster cocked his head, staring at her like an old friend. For the first few moments of hazy wakefulness, she could have sworn he was smiling at her.

"It's not polite to stare at a lady first thing in the morning," she said. "If you're going to stay in here to escape the cold, we need to teach you some manners."

She stood up and stretched her back. As she started walking, the rooster fluttered down from the bedpost and started marching along the cabin floor. He walked ahead of her, over to the two remaining pieces of firewood still propped by the stove, his little feet making surprisingly pleasant scratching sounds on the wooden floor.

Hannah checked the fire and found that it was down to slightly more than embers, so she stirred them and put one log in. When she closed the door, she saw Old Boreas right behind her, looking at her with that odd little tilt of his head.

"I don't suppose you're handy with an ax, are you?" she asked.

The rooster, naturally, had nothing to say.

Hannah set about throwing breakfast together. She used as little of her rations as possible, crafting up enough dough to make a respectable batch of biscuits. While she had them rising on top of the stove, she also warmed up some beans. It was then, as she looked at her meager collection of groceries, that she realized stove wood was not going to be her only issue in about three or four weeks.

She and Captain had some savings, but it wasn't much. And because he had left most of his money to his brother, Hannah knew she would have to start getting creative with her financial situation. She would not be at all surprised if the local bankers had decided to try to find some way to make sure she never got it.

When spring came, she would have to start her own vegetable garden. She was perfectly capable of creating and tending it. The small garden Captain had planted out back had shriveled up to dried dust. Then she thought about the Wishcaw, being down by the river, in the openness of the earth—maybe she could teach herself how to fish. Captain had taken her with him a time or two, and she knew the basics. Hunting crossed her mind as well, but the only gun Captain owned had fallen down that gorge with him. A rifle would cost money...that, and the fact that she had never even fired a rifle a single time in her life. She pushed that idea away like a rolling thunderstorm.

While she sorted all of this out in her head, she took inventory of the food she had, even counting the half bottle of old whiskey Captain had stowed in the farthest reaches of the cupboard. When she was done, her biscuits were just about ready, so she plucked two from the pan and had them with her beans. She was about halfway through her breakfast when her eyes wandered over to the space by the stove, which was just as empty as the space out back where she kept the firewood. If she didn't figure something out, she was going to be in for a rough season.

She looked down at her hands almost apologetically as this thought slowly consumed her. The very real fear of having to deal with this misery at least once a week settled in on her, and it was among the deepest dreads she had ever experienced.

Hannah looked back to the wood basket and the skimpy log on the floor and saw that Old Boreas was closely inspecting the area. He was nosing at a piece of bark, cocking his head this way and that when he suddenly looked up, locking eyes directly with her.

She had no misconceptions this time. Old Boreas *was* trying to communicate with her. He did not move his mouth, nor did he crack his dark beak open in any way. But somehow, he spoke to her.

She knew it was impossible, but it was very much what was taking place. Even though she knew stories of odd omens coming from animals was the stuff of old, insane spinsters, she *knew* it was happening.

"Let them," he said. *"Let them fear you."*

Rather than growing terrified that she was hearing the voice of a rooster in her head, Hannah instead focused on the words and what they meant. She thought of how the owner of the general store had treated her, and how that father had quickly ushered his child away from the counter when she approached. And how scared the teen boy had been when he'd brought those scraps of wood to her. And then there was

Emma Nichols, shooing Hannah away from her home as if she were diseased and refusing to sell her a pie.

Let them fear you.

Hannah looked to the stove and to the empty space beyond it. She knew what Old Boreas was hinting at, and it made a strange sort of sense. In fact, it stirred up an old childlike excitement within her.

"Yeah, I think you're right," she told the rooster. "I think you're right."

And though she was sure it was just a trick of her mind, a mind that was suddenly willing to accept that a rooster could be talking to her, no less, she was quite certain Old Boreas was inspiring her.

CHAPTER 15

She found the morning cold but not entirely unpleasant as she stepped out onto Crow Trail and headed toward town. In fact, when a very thin flurry of snow started to fall, she peered up into the gray sky and smiled. Watching the snow come down slowly reminded her of being a girl, catching flakes on her tongue or trapping them in her hand and watching them melt, only to slurp up the water they left behind.

Just before entering the town proper, a man driving a stagecoach passed by her and gave her a nasty look just out of the corner of his eye. She saw it all through a filter as the snow continued to fall, which almost made the man's agitated expression delightful. Hannah said nothing and responded in no certain way. She just kept walking into town. She had an agenda and intended to get to it without being distracted, so she carried on as the winter-stripped trees around Crow Trail fell away and revealed the sleepy, quiet town of Trumbull.

Let them fear you.

She heard the phrase over and over in her head, like musty wind howling through a cavern. Then something fell upon her like a thousand needles being poked at her skin. Hannah felt a reckoning, an awakening, and as a fiendish smile rose to her lips, she walked past a trio of women and a single man, altogether, who made no attempt to hide the fact that they were leering toward her, gawking her up and down. It was almost as if they did not trust her—as if they thought she might put a curse on them at any given moment. For perhaps the first time in her life, Hannah returned their gazes and stared right back at them, not in an antagonizing way, but almost as if she were warning them. When she smiled at them, all four people turned away from her at once.

She saw that the man with the wood cart was, again, nowhere to be found. However, the man she was *hoping* to find was easy to spot. He was sitting on the edge of the mercantile porch, looking to the space where the wood cart typically was. Hannah supposed he was trying to take advantage of the other man's absence, hoping to scoop up some of his loyal customers while he was away.

When the man's eyes fell on Hannah, he smiled and beckoned her over. Hannah hesitated for a moment, recalling their brief conversation from the day before when discussing his price for bringing her wood. *"If you're as full of evil as some people around here think you are, I imagine you'd be like fire in the bedroom. But I'd want it from behind... I can't bugger a widow if I can see her eyes."*

"You again, huh?" he said.

She nodded, unbuttoned her cloak, and approached him slowly. She adjusted her black bustle, pulling it down slightly to draw his eyes to her generous cleavage.

"You reconsidered my offer, I see?" he said, smiling, his rotting teeth on full display.

"I don't like it," she said, keeping her voice meek. "But, yes, I'll take your deal."

The man seemed confused for a moment, as if he were legitimately shocked that his tactic had worked. He regained his composure quickly, though, and now his smile was as wide as ever. It was clear this was not the first time he had ventured into such a deal with a desperate woman.

"Well, now, let's talk business," he said.

"Yes. Let's talk. I'm fine with your offer, but there's just a few things we need to change."

She had him hooked; she could see it in his eyes and the eager way his hands were moving aimlessly at his sides, and he could not keep his eyes off her breasts.

"Oh, you name it."

"I have no money to spare, so we can't go to the inn. I...

well, I will pay you when you deliver the wood to my cabin. And the other thing..." She stopped and stepped closer to him. This time she met his eyes. "It must be my mouth. Have you ever had a witch take you in her mouth? I hear it can be the most amazing feeling, it is almost nostalgic. That is what I hear anyway."

He chuckled and started adjusting himself in front of her. It seemed like he was priming himself for what was to come.

"Oh, we can work with that," he said. "But I don't think you're in any position to be making rules now, are you?"

"Oh, but it's not that *I* am making the rules," she said. She stepped even closer to him, and she could all but smell the lust coming out of his skin, warm and musky like overturned soil. "Have you not heard about me?" she whispered, so close that she knew he could smell her breath. "That there's something...something *wrong* with me? Something different? And if you lay with me like a man and woman are meant to lay together, I can promise that the poison will spread." She quickly glanced at his eyes to see if he believed her, but it was hard to tell. The lust in his eyes was far too prominent to see much of anything else. "But the things I can do with my mouth," she went on, "might be safer for you. I don't think the poison can spread that way. But I can't be sure..."

"The hell you say!"

She shook her head slowly and met his eyes. This time, she projected more confidence than she had managed to muster since Captain had died. It was almost like something else was guiding her, something dark and devious.

"Hell," she said, and snickered coquettishly. "I figure you'll learn all about that one way or the other. You bring me that wood, because if you don't...well, I guess you can get used to those so-called pew people around here giving you mean looks just like they give me, because that will be their punishment. But mine will be far worse. I guarantee your skin will fall off and everyone will know." Hannah poked at his chest, staring perniciously at his crotch. "Maybe something else." Her hands rested securely on her bustier, adjusting it back to shape. Pushing her hair away from her cheeks and inhaled with high proficient. "Bring me that wood."

The man backed away, shaking his head. "You bitch!" he said. "You get away from me, you damn witch!"

"Of course," she said, stepping away. "But you bring me that wood. And if you want the payment afterward, you can come and get it. It's your decision. Either way, we should spit and shake on it. If not, treasure your wood, health, and anything else you see sacred. Because I swear, the wrath of darkness will fall upon you."

She left him staring at her, completely aghast. She offered him one last smile before she turned away and started back down the road. When she had left Trumbull behind her, she allowed herself to revel in the thrill and power of what she had just done. Never in all her life had she caused anyone—much less a man—to strike such a posture of fear. In her mind, she could still see his eyes widening with alarm as the desire for her shrank away, only to be replaced by fear and worry.

The question, of course, was whether it had worked. She knew it was a gamble that might cost her dearly if it failed. But something dark, something accursed, tore through her mind, "You will not fail." But the mere thought of those deep, dark winter nights without a warm cabin sent a promise of aching pain through her. She looked down at her hands, the pain was easing. The bones subsided and she stared curious at them, they looked as smooth and healthy as they did before her mother had brought the hammer down on them. Hannah felt vindicated as she smiled.

As she continued down Crow Trail, she wasn't aware of it, but she had stopped in front of the Nichols property. The girls were not out in the yard, and there was no scent of pies in the air. It was odd, because the still-falling flurries seemed to literally call out for both—the laughter of children and the crisp smell of something freshly baked to cut through the cold.

Still, stirred by her performance in town, Hannah turned into the yard and walked to the front porch as if Emma Nichols herself had given her the invitation to do so. When she climbed the stairs and knocked on the door, she did so with confidence. She had already worked up a smile to greet whoever answered the door.

THE WITCH OF MONROE

As she assumed, it was Emma. The youngest daughter gripped her mother's leg and smiled, peering out from behind Emma. Emma shook her head and let out an exasperated sigh. There was flour on her hands and apron, indicating that she had been in the middle of preparing food of some kind. Maybe the winter air would be tinged with the smell of apple pies this day after all.

Before Hannah could say anything, Emma started. "Now, Hannah, I'm a godly woman, and I try really hard to accommodate the needs of everyone as I can. But the last time we spoke, didn't we tell you to leave us be?"

"You did," Hannah said, keeping the smile on her face. "And I'm very sorry, Mrs. Nichols, I really am. But to tell you the truth, I've been thinking about an apple pie ever since I smelled yours the last time I came by. I sure would appreciate it if you'd sell me one."

"I said no yesterday and I'm saying no now. Now you get on, Hannah Cranna. I really don't want to have to get the law involved in this."

Hannah Cranna, she thought. But Hannah nodded, as if she understood perfectly. "Is it because you're such a godly woman? Is that why you won't deal with me? Is this what your God teaches? To be mean spirited toward those in need?"

Emma's brow furrowed as she started to close the door. "You'll not mock my faith, young lady!"

"Oh, I'm not, I promise. But I am your neighbor, and

I am in need. My husband is dead, and everyone in this miserable little town turns their noses up at me because they're all convinced I killed him. And it looks like that includes you, too."

Emma looked furious and drew back to completely shut the door right in Hannah's face.

"If I came to the so-called Jesus you claim to love, I wonder what He would say? I suppose He would turn your water into wine and rot your fruit at the sight of hunger, wouldn't He?

Hannah watched as Emma paused. When Emma looked back at Hannah, there were tears in her eyes. As one escaped, Emma quickly wiped it away, leaving a streak of white flour across her cheek. Hannah wondered if the woman was upset because someone had the nerve to attack her faith, or if she cried out of nothing more than pure fear.

Let them fear you. Hannah smiled again.

"Wait right here," Emma Nichols said.

Hannah watched curiously as the woman closed the door. She could hear Emma scolding her youngest daughter for smiling at the "bad woman" who was visiting. Hannah waited for a few minutes, wondering if Old Boreas was right. She knew he was. Fear was a tool more powerful than a musket on a battlefield and a lot quicker to load, and Hannah was quickly learning how to use it. She had to be patient but resolute in her demands. So she waited and listened as Emma moved through the house. Her steps sounded like a herd of horses pounding on the floors. When the door finally opened again, Emma was holding an old, battered pie-tin. A small white towel covered the top, but the smell was unmistakable: an apple pie.

"It's already missing a slice, but this is all I have left," Emma said, thrusting the pie out to Hannah. "Take it."

Hannah did, gladly, and with the same thin smile on her face, she knew she had won again. "How much?"

"Nothing. You...you may have evil in you, but you're right. Plus, it's made with winter apples and not as sweet but still decent." Emma Nichols steadied herself a bit before she went on, her voice remaining thick and confident. "As a woman of the Lord, it is my duty to help my fellow men when they are in need. But please, Hannah, you can't keep coming here."

Hannah peeked under the towel and looked at the pie. It was still flaky, and the interior was thick and gooey, making her mouth water. "Thank you, Emma."

And in the same way she had dismissed the man back in town, Hannah turned away from Emma and walked down the steps. She was humming softly to herself when she got back to the road, taking in the smell of the pie. It was so enticing that even before she reached home, Hannah dug into it with her bare hands and started to eat it.

CHAPTER 16

Dinner consisted of the remainder of the biscuits with a few strips of salted meat. As Hannah enjoyed them, it occurred to her that finding meat for the winter was going to be quite a task. Though Captain had been considered somewhat financially stable, he had not owned an ice chest. Instead, he rented out space in one of the chests at the general store, sharing it with a few others, and she figured it was safe to assume that she would no longer be able to utilize that space. With no ice chest, the only way to eat meat was going to be to cook it rather soon after the meat was captured. She knew how to salt meat to help preserve it for a time, but that would only go so far.

Once again, she thought of fishing. It would be almost torture to do it with the weather so cold, but she knew it would probably come to that. She also recalled Captain setting traps for rabbits and foxes, which they had eaten every now and then. Chasing after rabbits was, as she understood it, among the reasons he had died falling off that damned gorge. This brought a smile to Hannah's lips. She wasn't sure how to make the traps, but figured it was rather simple. Maybe she could trap a hare or two. After all, she supposed she had plenty of time to work on such talents.

Old Boreas strutted his way around the cabin while she ate. He approached her feet and looked up at her. She tossed a meager crumb of bread down onto the floor for him. "I think it might have worked," she said as she slid her plate away and pulled Emma's apple pie over. "I think we might be—"

The sound of squeaking wheels and the soft clatter of horse hooves interrupted her. They were very close by, likely at the very edge of her yard, so she went to the window and looked out. Sure enough, the man from town was pulling a small wagon with a rather respectable pile of wood on it. Smiling, Hannah turned to Old Boreas.

"We got wood!" she said, leaning down, scratching at his head before heading to the front door.

Dusk was only about an hour away, and the cold was settling in rapidly. The snow had stopped falling about an hour before, but the fat gray clouds loomed like boulders overhead and promised much more. She shivered against the cold as she watched the man bring the horse to a stop. When he saw Hannah, he seemed to look just slightly away from her, as if he were talking to the side of the cabin rather than to her. She knew he was afraid, the stench of fear smelled like rotting meat and somehow, Hannah sensed every part of it.

"Where do you want it?" he asked.

"Around back. You'll see where the other wood used to be." She tilted her head and grinned. "And what about your payment?"

He looked away quickly, toward the back of the cabin. "Just a buck or two, I reckon," he said. "If you want, I can come by every two weeks or so and make sure you don't run out."

She gave him a curt, businesslike nod. "That will be just fine."

The man whipped the horse into motion and steered it to the back of the cabin while Hannah went inside and took two dollars from the candy tin. "You think this is too much?" she asked Old Boreas as he watched her every move. He pecked two times at the floor and followed her closely when she went back to the door and opened it. She could feel the black rooster watching her as she placed the two dollars on the bottom porch step. She lingered a bit, listening to the sound of the man at work behind the cabin. The soft thudding noise and occasional clicking sound of wood being stacked seemed to warm her heart more than any fire ever could. She looked back at Old Boreas. "It should be a fine payment." The rooster pecked again and continued to watch her.

When she went back inside, she stayed by the window until the wagon was pulled back across her yard. The bit of snow that had gathered on the ground during the flurries of the day showed the path of his progress to and from her yard. As the man headed back into Trumbull with dusk not too far behind, Hannah laughed heartily, as if someone had told her some great joke. It came out of nowhere and actually startled her a bit at first, but then both her lungs and heart leaned into it, and the laughter came even harder and with more joy.

Looking through the window at the approaching night, she continued to laugh and, when she was able to draw a proper breath, she uttered four words that were beginning to rotate in her head like a chant, maybe a prayer.

"Let them fear you."

CHAPTER 17

Winter gave up any pretense of seeming calm, gentle, or kind about two weeks later. The first heavy snow came ten days after the delivery of the firewood, and the temperatures plummeted after that. Hannah was able to keep the cabin warm thanks to the sizable pile of wood she now had out back, and because of the warmth, her hands did not present the hellish problem she had been expecting. Even when they did flare up and reminded her of just how painful they could be, she had plenty of the medicine she had gotten from O'Keeffe's at the start of winter.

Since the temperatures remained below freezing, the snow remained like a veil, covering everything. Some mornings she would wake up to find not only a new blanket of snow on the ground, but a layer of frost that had accumulated on the snowless nights. Even when the skies were not dumping inches of snow on Trumbull, the freezing temperatures were doing their own special sort of damage.

This made Hannah reluctant to go out. Not that she had anywhere to go. As a result, she spent eleven days not doing much of anything in the cabin. She read from some of the books she and Captain had acquired during their time together while sitting as close to the wood stove as she could stand. She started reading Charles Dickens' The Pickwick Papers then summoned the courage to read The Vampyre instead. Hannah did not scare easily, but the mere idea of exploring the endless amounts of darkness all around horrified her. The narrow avenues a man so sophisticated could control so many due to fear...it was mortifying and pleasurable at the same time.

Through it all, Old Boreas remained in the cabin with her, watching her and studying her every move. He would, on occasion, go over to the front door and peck at it. Hannah would let him out, and he would come back to the door about fifteen minutes later, pecking to be let inside. She assumed he did this to go outside and relieve himself because she never saw any signs that he had done so inside the cabin.

After those eleven days of solitude because of the frost and snow, the sun finally presented itself again. It shone brightly up in the sky but offered little more than a weak thaw. Hannah waited another day before convincing herself to head into town. She still had enough food, though she would hesitate to use the word "plenty," and at least another six- or seven-days' worth of wood.

Finally, Hannah wrapped her cloak around her shoulders, smiled at Old Boreas, and left the cabin. She knew she needed eggs and milk, maybe some fresh meat if they had it. Any meat would do, really, since the only meat she'd had since Captain's passing nearly eight weeks before were the salted meat strips. While they were quite delicious, they didn't do much in the way of fulfilling her craving. She also planned to stop by the mercantile to see if she could find some books or other resources that might teach her how to properly fish. She figured she could spend the long, isolated winter days reading up on the craft and then put her knowledge to use when spring came back around.

Perhaps it was the snow, or the small victories she had achieved just before the snowfall in the way of stove wood and apple pie, but the town felt different. The air seemed fresher somehow, and Hannah did not feel as if she were swimming against some unseen tide. It had nothing to do with the attitudes of the people she saw. No, they were still reluctant to look at her, and many even crossed over to the other side of the street if they saw her coming their way. She wasn't certain, but she also thought she saw a woman subtly making the shape of a cross with her two forefingers as she came out of the post office.

Hannah found things much the same at the grocer's as well. There were a few people inside when she went in, and she didn't even make it to the first shelf before the grocer cut her off. He looked absolutely mortified, and when he placed his hand on her shoulder to lead her back out onto the porch, he reacted as if he had placed his hand on hot iron. He moved quickly, but never removed his hand until they were standing in the cold.

"Mrs. Hovey, I told you I can't have you in here."

"Yes, you told me you'd deliver things to the back door, but that's just ridiculous and I will not stand for it."

"Stand for it? That's your problem, ma'am," he said, eyeing Hannah. "I said to send a list and drop it off at the back door. That's all I can do for you."

Refusing to buckle under his heated stare and anger, she kept her chin high. "Should I do that right now, then?" she asked with an edge of bitterness to her voice. "Would you like me to write a list and leave it at the back door?"

"No. People have already seen... By God, just tell me what you want, and I'll have it all at the back in fifteen minutes. Leave your money and take your things."

"This town is full of foul pigs!" Hannah said, stepping forward. Her eyes were menacing black, and her pupils were no longer perceptible. The grocer stepped back, trying to get space between him and Hannah. He finally stopped when he felt his back rest against the door. "And do you know what happens to foul pigs? The whole herd gets infested. Treasure your store, Mr. Mean, Meanie Man! Treasure your health, and all these people. I see dreadful darkness coming your way and to everyone else in this damn town. Damn you I say, damn it all."

"Mrs. Hovey, j-just tell me what you want."

"I want eggs, milk, and meat," she said, then felt a joy grow inside of her as she heard his voice crack and shake with every word as he responded.

"I-I have no milk. The rest I can get you. I have some chickens that the butcher did not want. I can get it fo-for you."

"Good." Hannah patted him on his shoulder. "You do just that," she said.

The grocer exhaled, turning his face from Hannah. She stepped back and saw his hands twitching along with his knees. As they buckled underneath him, Hannah smiled. There were so many things she wanted to say, so much fury building up inside of her. The mantra that had become so encouraging was swirling in her head like angry wasps.

Hannah watched as the grocer stumbled back inside. As she waited, she felt eyes fall upon her. It was like an awakening. When she turned back around, she saw that her presence had attracted a crowd. There were several people standing either on the side of the road or right in the middle of it, gaping at her. There were many things she wanted to say, many accusatory statements loaded and ready like rounds in a gun. Instead, she tilted her head at them.

"Good day, all." Her brow lifted and she felt her eyes bore through them like venom.

As they started to turn away, she saved a smile with just a touch of evil for the last few who kept their eyes on her for just a moment longer than the others. It was a smile of mischief, the smile of someone who may just be keeping a very devilish secret.

Something squeaked behind her, and the grocer stood in the doorway with her food. She stared curiously at him, and he handed her the bag, but did not speak. Hannah took the supplies with just enough menace in her eyes that the grocer took a step back and closed the door. She felt triumph as she made her way to the mercantile store for fishing supplies, then headed back home along the partially frozen and muddy tracks of Crow Trail.

She passed three people in carriages and one man on horseback. No one spoke to her, a recently widowed woman lugging two bags of groceries and supplies along the messy road. Apparently, Emma Nichols was the only one who took the "Love thy neighbor" business somewhat seriously. It made her wonder just how dark and vile she would have to become. She wondered about the stories that were whispered about her in dark rooms as children tried to frighten one another, and as the older folks spoke of demons and witches and the devil. This made her giggle slightly, and she hummed a tune in her head and noticed her feet began to skip a bit as she headed home. Hannah was happy.

Back at the cabin, she sat at the kitchen table and looked through the book on fishing she had picked up in town. She read about knots, practicing them on loose bits of yarn rather than wasting the actual fishing line itself. And as she read and practiced, Old Boreas watched with great interest from the floor.

That night she had a dinner of chicken, biscuits, and beans. It was the best she had eaten since Captain had died. She looked to the side of the table he used to occupy and felt a deep, longing of happiness. She knew full well that she would not weep for him any longer, nor would she put her life on pause for him. But she had known him well, and he would be furious if he knew how she was being treated in town.

She imagined him laying into the grocer, correcting him on how a lady should be treated, then coming back home and taking his frustrations out on her. That was Captain's way, and it was a way Hannah grew to know early on in their marriage. Just a week after they'd married, Captain came home from hunting empty-handed, blamed Hannah for God turning away from him, and tied her to the bedposts for three days to punish her. He had whipped her nightly with his belt. She remembered how his hardened hands had always been so soft, yet expert at making the transition from gentle and caring to grasping and urgent. She thought of his hands on her and closed her eyes.

It's been over eight weeks since you've known his touch and his pain. I don't believe he would mind... she heard Old Boreas whisper.

Before the thought had fully formed, her hands were trailing down the valley between her breasts. And when they reached lower and tickled her clit, she was arching her back against the chair, crying out to a man who was no longer there. She reached a form of ecstasy. She wished he could watch her, see her happiness without him, her pleasure. As she moaned louder, she untied her bustier, exposing her firm breasts and rubbing her nipples between her fingers. A small burst of wind blew through the cabin as her hair flayed across her cheeks. She felt something separating her knees, pulling her legs apart, wider, but Hannah did not care as the pleasure tore through her body like a blade. She gasped a name that entered her mind, *Boreas,* and whispers bounced off the walls of her cabin, echoing in her ears. *Give me your hands, Hannah. Give me the one you used to touch yourself. Are you a whore, Hannah?*

She nearly fell out of the chair, and when she opened her eyes, for just a moment, she had seen him. A flickering image in the corner, she did not who he was, but his black boots covered in mud and muck. He was standing, staring, watching her at play. Rather than feeling fear at this realization, she felt oddly secure. She felt desired and wanted, even though it was just for a moment, Hannah felt safe.

Old Boreas strutted from the bedroom, fluttering his wings, cawing in triumph. Hannah wondered what was wrong with him as his black feathers separated and one floated across the cabin, landing at Hannah's feet. He stood and watched her. His small, piercing eyes devoured her. Hannah bent down and picked up the gift Old Boreas had given her, smelling it, rubbing it softly across her cheeks and then down the center of her breast. She inhaled deeply, and as their eyes met, Hannah got a better understanding of her rooster. He was becoming her familiar.

CHAPTER 18

The temperature dropped fifteen degrees two days later. Hannah was aware of it the moment she woke up. Though the cabin had been warmed by the fire, her hands were fairly screaming with pain. She tried making fists of them, and she was able to do so, but only with great effort.

She sat up on the edge of the bed for a moment, her feet dangling toward the floor. She felt the heat from the wood stove, but it was slight—not because the fire was dead or dying, but because it was just so damned cold.

"It's going to be one of those days, Old Boreas," she said.

Hannah heard the rooster clucking somewhere in the house. When she walked near the hearth, she saw him strutting by the front door. He regarded her for a moment, then pecked at the door to go out. She opened the door and looked at the wintry landscape before her. Snow was still on the ground, crusted with a bit of frost. The stripped trees looked like wobbling supports for the sky. The morning was so quiet that she could hear the complaints of those trees, griping about their snowy burden. The silence left behind by the ice and snow was like that of a tomb. She closed her eyes and listened to the absolute wall of nothing that greeted her.

After taking in a deep breath of the crisp air, she walked back into the cabin, leaving Old Boreas to his business. She took some of the tonic for her hands and had a lazy breakfast of oats and half of a leftover biscuit. She heard Boreas scratching at the door again, and she opened it. He shuffled back in and ruffled his feathers a bit. The cold had apparently gotten to him too.

Hannah watched him as he made a series of circles around her. They were slow and methodical, she thought, yet with purpose. Odd behavior for a rooster, she supposed. Maybe he was just trying to keep himself warm by staying in motion.

The day passed in a boring, frigid expanse—one of those cold winter days that seemed to freeze even the passage of time. Hannah experimented with fishing knots. It was no easy task since her fingers and joints still felt stiff. Then she read passages about the different kinds of fish in the area.

She read about brook trout, crappie, and an assortment of different bass fish. She realized that, at some point, she was going to have to figure out how to properly scale and gut the damned things, too. Hannah was so into her new adventure of fishing that when a sudden sharp *bang* sounded out against the side of her house, she hardly noticed.

But when it came again, Old Boreas scurried around in the kitchen like the little soldier he was, rushing to the door to be let out. Hannah heard a strange, deep throaty sound coming from him as his little feet scratched and clicked along the floor. Hannah slowly made her way over to the window to look out onto the front yard when the sound came again. This time, it was more like a *whap!*

Hannah's eyes widened curiously when she saw three young children at the edge of her yard, throwing rocks and snowballs toward her cabin. There were two boys and a girl, all around the age of nine or ten. They stood at the very edge of her yard, not doing much to hide themselves. One of the boys was staring in the direction of the cabin, forming a snowball in his hands, while the other two children were just behind him, playfully tossing handfuls of snow at one another. The sight of it made her furious and she felt heat radiating in her temples, making them throb.

"Little bastards!" Hannah said as she grabbed her cloak and walked out onto the porch. Old Boreas was right by her side.

When Hannah moved closer to the porch steps, all three of the children froze in place. She could see the smaller of the two boys readying his feet to run away, back through the woods toward Trumbull, but the older boy and the girl stood their ground. And when Hannah leaned down and whispered something to Old Boreas, the children sprinted back through the forest like a lightning bolt across a summer sky. Hannah laughed out loud when the little girl screamed, "She has a devil!"

"You have no idea! Your little skin shall boil, you varmint kids!" Hannah yelled, and Old Boreas cawed so loud that his cries echoed off the floor of the forest and bounced all the way to Wayman's Gorge.

Hannah spied them cautiously. She nearly called out to them. She could only imagine what would be said about the incident in town. But as she did, she heard a familiar statement in her voice. It sounded like a hissing serpent in an abandoned hall.

Your skin shall boil, she whispered.

For a moment, her heart seemed to fight this. Her instincts told her to give chase. But the echo of that voice grew louder and, before she knew it, Hannah started walking forward. As she did, Old Boreas followed. She grinned at the sight of the fleeing children. Running and screaming, they entered the tree line and tore through the woods. Hannah could hear the girl's voice. This was not a scream of pain, but of fear. It carried up and out over the treetops in the frigid silence of the day. It warmed Hannah more than she would have expected.

But then Hannah saw...*something*. Some great shape, lumbering through the trees, not quite transparent but also not made of anything substantial at all. There was no definite form, no limbs or appendages, but *something* was out there, and it was on the move. It almost looked as if the wind had taken on some sort of form and was tearing harmlessly through the trees on the heels of the children.

Hannah remained in her yard and watched as the shape grew closer and closer. She heard the girl scream again and then...silence. The forest was asleep.

Hannah stood there, probing the liquid form as it moved through the woods, turning and weaving in and out of the trees toward her cabin. When it reached the tree line, Hannah stepped forward, walking slowly toward the forest. When she looked back, Old Boreas was gone. Hannah had no idea what it was before her, but she did not fear it. She sensed that she had been aware of it before, lurking out back along the edges of her property where the woodpile sat. If anything, it gave her a strange level of security as she moved forward. She removed her cloak as she entered the forest, wondering what was calling for her.

Emma Nichols had gone through two bags of winter apples trying to cut enough for an apple pie when she heard the most gut-wrenching scream coming from outside. She knew Rube had taken the girls to the grocer in town for a few items they needed, so she knew it was not them. Still, she dropped her knife, wiped her hands, and ran outside to see where the noise came from.

Emma reached the edge of her yard and looked up and down Crow Trail. At first, she did not see anyone, but she continued to hear screams coming from the forest. She stepped into the muddy road and stretched her eyes up Crow Trail in both directions. Toward town, it looked abandoned, with no one in sight. As she turned her head toward Hannah's cabin, she saw a dark figure cross into the forest. Emma watched and felt something stir inside as she too shot across the road and entered the forest, walking secretly toward the Wishcaw River.

Emma walked to the edge of the clearing and eyed the dead brush, sweeping it back with her hands. She was careful on the frozen patches of the ground and examined each path that led her away from her house and into the midst of the forest. Overhead she noticed the snow clouds breaking up, and for a moment she prayed for the sun to appear. Maybe it would show the way toward the river. Emma had never been this deep into the forest. Normally that was Rube's job, and he always told her how easy it was to get turned around in the dark secrets of the woods. But something inside urged her to move deeper into the brush.

She heard the scrambling of footsteps coming right toward her, like a herd of horses escaping from their captors. It was three children, running with their mouths agape and screaming louder than she had ever heard a child scream. The bigger of the boys slammed right into Emma, nearly knocking her down. Tears flowed down his cheeks. It was mixed with blood from scratches etched into his pale skin by the brush.

"What is it?" Emma asked as the boy wrapped his arms around her, shaking with fear. The boy looked up at Emma and she noticed large blisters rapidly firing around his eyes and moving down toward his cheeks. He raised his fragile hands and pointed toward Hannah's house but still did not speak. Emma looked at the other boy and saw that he, too, was suffering. Welts covered his arms and neck, simmering and festering all over his skin. She recognized the girl from church and the pharmacy. She thought her name was Mary. Mary O'Keeffe. Her father had been the pharmacist in Trumbull for a very long time.

"Mary! Mary, what happened to you? What is going on?" Emma asked as she watched bright blood and puss flow from Mary's mouth. Boils ravished her tongue, and the girl was unable to speak. Mary walked toward Emma like the world had some sort of interference and she was having a hard time playing catchup. She was troubled and distracted. Her eyes were wide with no reflection in them whatsoever. She wobbled on her feet, her eyes staring straight through Emma.

"Mary?" Emma asked again. "OK, listen, you all run home, run fast, all of you. Got it? Go on! Get!" The kids took off through the forest heading toward Trumbull. Emma watched them until they disappeared in the distance and wondered what had happened to them. They ran as if they were giving chase and losing at every turn. She shook the thought out of her mind and peered through the trees, stepping slowly, and watching.

The closer she got to the river, the more the naked trees moved in a restless manner on both sides of the trail. The bright clouds overhead pushed across the sky, leaving dark billows of mass in their wake. The wind picked up and blew violently. Emma put her head down, protecting her face as snow blasted by her like a twister. She shuddered, and despite her desire to turn around and get back to the safety of her own house, she rapidly moved forward, deeper into the forest.

When she got about twenty feet from Wayman's Gorge, she took a sharp turn heading toward the place she thought Hannah would be. Dead leaves crunched beneath her feet from the ice and snow. The fallen vegetation seemed to have a life of its own, dead things with nothing to do. When Emma got closer to the river, she saw her. Hannah was twirling around in sync with the forest.

Emma walked slowly, trying not to get Hannah's attention. She watched from behind a giant oak tree as Hannah lay by the creek's edge. Her shoulders dug into the dead leaves, and she was drunk on the brightness of the sun. For Emma, it was such an extraordinary vision. Hannah's long black curls flared out like angel wings, but Emma knew she did not look like the angels described in her Bible. In the Good Book, the women were mostly pasty with yellow hair and fair eyes and dressed in silk and satin, colors as bright as the sun. Their skin was clear and soft, with ravishing cheeks. Emma thought Hannah was neither of those. She was different.

Emma shuffled her feet and looked around. She cringed when she noticed a few slithering serpents that hung from the brush around Hannah. The trees began to creak with the wind as it blew between them, singing its performance of the winter season. Dead leaves showered down all around her. Her eyes widened as Hannah raised her hands and listened to the sounds of the dusky forest. Suddenly, multiple rows of encrusted vines twisted up from the muddy ground like bony fingers, all reaching toward Hannah and scratching her skin.

Emma had never realized how beautiful Hannah was. The bones of her face were so sharp, it looked as if she were carved out of stone. Whispers seemed to be falling as softly as feathers on the floor of the forest, and as the sound of them reached Emma's ears, her skin began to crawl, and her eyes glazed over. Cold beads of sweat formed in the crease between her breasts, it felt as though she was bathing in it.

Hannah continued to whisper, and the wind around Emma shifted quickly, roaring wildly. Remnants of dead things swirled madly, but she did not budge. The whispers continued to echo through the forest, and Emma felt a chill run down her spine as the ground beneath her trembled. Scrambling footsteps pierced her ears, and the clouds shifted quickly as darkness rolled across the skies like thunder.

Emma! Touch yourself, Emma!

The whispers appeared all around, striking Emma like a bolt of lightning. She felt a presence, yet when she turned, no one was there. A sigh of relief escaped her mouth as she turned back toward Hannah and saw that she was on her knees, talking. But the space around her remained vacant. Emma watched as the trees leaned in like a canopy, paying homage to Hannah as she spoke to them with words that Emma could not understand. For a moment, Emma's eyes narrowed, and she swore she saw something dark and fiendish radiating around Hannah. Then Hannah reached up and caressed her neck, groping her breasts, touching herself in ways that Emma knew Christian women did not do.

Emma's body was aware of her response to it. She was drawn into the action and found that she was touching herself in the same places. First her breasts, tickling her nipples. They were erect through her house dress, and she continued to tease them. When Hannah's fingers strayed between her thighs...Hannah laughed, and Emma closed her eyes and moaned, reaching under her own dress, and plunging her fingers into ecstasy. She touched herself in ways she was not used to. It was a yearning––a need that was completely foreign to her. She knew she should flee and run back to the comfort of her house where Jesus lived and she was safe, but those reasons fled her mind as soon as they appeared. She was intoxicated. She wanted this. She wanted to watch, to be possessed by the images of Hannah. Hannah was making her feel something she had never felt before, and now she was hungry for it. Emma opened her eyes, and the forest was silent. Hannah was no longer there. The trees were undisturbed, and the ground was covered in powder from the snow. The ground lay undisturbed, with no sign of Hannah ever being there. Emma stared curiously at what she saw. Then she pulled her dress down, pushed herself away from the oak, and ran quickly back through the forest toward her cabin.

Drunk on the afternoon's events, Emma felt satisfied. With every sound of her footsteps, she looked curiously at the ground as dead leaves crunched beneath her feet. The forest sang to her, and the whispers filled her ears, singing in sync...

There are no devils.

CHAPTER 19

The winter passed sluggishly, and when it made its way out, it did so in a particularly ugly fashion. It dropped another nine inches of snow on the town of Trumbull and the surrounding areas for about fifty or sixty miles in all directions. Blessedly, the temperatures that followed were not nearly as cold and vicious as the first go-round. This was good news for Hannah, but miserable news for anyone planning to get out and about. The thaw of the snow created thin, shallow rivers, one of which seemed to start directly at the mouth of Hannah's yard before working its way down Crow Trail toward town.

Old Boreas stayed inside with Hannah almost every day. After the Constable paid a visit, asking about the incident with the children in the woods, Hannah began to feel a more solid connection to the rooster. She knew he was her familiar, and she thought he sensed it as well. She knew he was doing what he could to thwart the visitors when the whispers began to become clearer. *Careful, Hannah,* he repeated as the balding man stood on her porch and questioned her about the incident with an accusing tongue. He explained to Hannah that the three children, including little Mary O'Keeffe, were suffering from a plague after playing near her house. Hannah remembered laughing at the accusations and shooing him off her property. He threatened court action and warned her that the church might get involved in the matter. That was when Old Boreas cawed at him, and the man ran as fast as he could to his carriage. Hannah was sure it would not be the last of the visitors, but for now, she would just have to wait.

As for Old Boreas, she knew the longer they stayed together, the safer she felt. She found herself talking to him more and more. He was preparing her for what was to come. She would tell him her inner thoughts, stories about Captain and about her childhood a bit farther south, where tobacco fields had started to take over most of Virginia. She told him about stealing blackberries from the neighbor's vines, and how she used to capture toads and place them in her mother's cot for spite. She also told him about growing up in an encampment with other later-to-the-party settlers, and how it was there that she had first seen a man get killed, a woman raped, and where she first had the thought that there was a very accessible devil in the world.

She never spoke about what her mother had done to her, though. There were some things she dared not conjure up to explore. But part of her knew Old Boreas already knew. She knew there were some evils that were too close to her. Through it all, Boreas always seemed to listen, cocking his head to the left and right, and at times she thought she heard him speak back.

That had been weeks ago. And the more she tried to recall the moments, the clearer it seemed. Still, every now and then Old Boreas would look at her as if he knew something she did not—as if he had a deep, delicious secret that he was just waiting for her to discover. She couldn't help but wonder if that was why he was there. Maybe he had come to her, or someone had sent him. She often wondered if he had come because he had a message for her and was simply waiting for the right time to convey it. Some afternoons, when dusk settled around the cabin and another cold night lurked like a monster in the frigid distance, that was exactly the energy she got from him.

At the end of February, though, winter was still in the air. The temperatures seemed to suggest that spring was coming to call. Still, there were chilly, bitter mornings, and Hannah was constantly checking her supply of firewood. Her hands seemed to be more comfortable once January saw its way out, but the pains were still there. They became more manageable, and she still had enough tonic to last awhile, so it was no real concern just yet.

The rather crude gentleman who had propositioned her at the start of winter had come by four times during those cold, difficult months. Each time, he would stop in the yard to make his presence known, and Hannah would place his money on her front stoop. No words were ever exchanged between them, and that seemed to suit the man just fine, based on the speed with which he usually guided his horse out of the yard. It was a very simple, yet effective business model.

It was during that final stretch of February the man bringing her firewood, came by for the fifth time. The roads, particularly Crow Trail, were still muddy and ruined, but they were drastically better than when the thaw had first occurred. The horse pulled the cart much easier through the yard.

As she watched from her door, the man avoided eye contact and gave her a curt little nod. She watched him guide the horse, his arms filling the long sleeves of his shirt to a nice, tight fit. He was a plainly handsome man, a feature she had not noticed when she'd first met him, but now, almost five months removed from Captain's funeral, she allowed herself to think about what it might be like to be with another man.

Hannah had always enjoyed sex and the exploration of

sensuality, and she had often been adventurous and playful with it. She had been interested in it from a young age, despite her mother's punishments upon finding that Hannah had been, as her mother had referred to it, touching herself. So, for her, the thought of bedding a man, any man, wasn't as taboo as some in Trumbull might think. In fact, the more she thought of it and watched the man guide the cart to the back, the more she wanted it. And the more she knew she had to have it.

It was an urge that had only crept along her nerves a few times since Captain had died, and when she felt it, she had handled things by herself in a very adventurous way. Now, though, she needed more. It wasn't just a physical need, but some sort of aching mental want—not of intimacy, but some bizarre thing that Hannah could not quite name. It was not lust; it was nothing that simple. It went beyond physical need and leaned toward something spiritual.

She walked onto the porch and waited for him to come back around. She listened to the sounds of him stacking wood: the creaking of the cart, the knocking of the pieces of wood together, and his occasional grunt of effort. Her mind conjured images of work-worn hands on her body, of breath on her neck and breasts. She instantly placed Captain's face to the imagery, but even now, as her body started to truly crave a man's touch, that face was flickering and distant. It did not need to be Captain. Honestly, it didn't even have to be the man currently stacking the wood. It could be anyone, she did not care. Hannah could not remember ever feeling such a powerful sexual urge in her life, but she was nearly overcome with it. Her head was swimmy, and her knees were like jelly. Odder still, it had come out of nowhere. It had been little more than a flickering flame when the man had pulled the cart into the yard, but somehow, it had turned into a raging fire that she could feel blistering between her legs. It was a pulse screaming to her, a rapidly building heat that she could not get a grip on. She was growing impossibly wet, and it became an act of will and an effort not to go out and approach the man in that very moment.

Suddenly, the wheels of the cart creaking back toward the front yard echoed in her ears, and she readied herself. She felt the cold creep into her bones as the sweat narrowing down between her breasts sent a shiver on her skin. She had the idea to strip down completely nude before he came around the side of the house. The mere idea of it only strengthened her desire. The image of her naked body waiting in the cold, with her flesh turning pink with goosebumps, was feeding her craving.

The horse came marching around the side of the cabin, the cart jostling along behind it. The man sat at the front, and his eyes instantly fell on her. He was looking low at first, at the porch step where she usually left his payment, but this time she had the money in her hand and fully intended to give it to him one way or the other. Overtaken by her own desires, she stood waiting, naked beneath her thin white house dress.

With the slightest bit of hesitation to his movements, the man halted the horse and met her eyes. "Ma'am," he said, tilting his head.

"Good evening." She fumbled with the money in her hand and held it out to him. He didn't move at first, staring at her from head to toe as if she were a tree that had miraculously come to life and started speaking. But she also saw a flicker of the stubbornness and determination most men have in them, the reluctance to appear scared or uncertain. He ordered the horse to stay and stepped down from the bench, holding steady eye contact with her breasts as he moved slowly toward her. Her nipples swelled and hardened under the steady gaze of his big sparkling eyes. Hannah felt a sudden tightness between her legs as the moisture there grew. She felt her tongue touch her lips.

"Th-This should be the last you'll need for the season," he said. "Warmer days are just weeks ahead. If you need more, just...well, you know where to find me."

She handed him the money, and he reached for it graciously. When their hands met, she gently took his fingers and tugged playfully at them.

"I appreciate all you've done. And if you still want the original price, you asked for, I believe you've earned it."

The look of surprise that came across his face was

almost childlike. She saw a smile start to break his lips, and he took a step forward. As he drew closer to her, his desire was apparent, but then he hesitated. Without any sort of warning, he looked away from her and yanked his hand away.

"What are you doing to me?" he asked. "I feel not myself."

"Not yourself?" Hannah said with a smile. "Before, you said you liked the idea, remember? Standing firm with your cock out. Wanting to bed a witch and all. From behind, of course. That's how you like it, correct? Now I want to give it to you."

"No, no way in hell I'm gonna do that. I heard what you did to those kids, with their skin and all."

"Kids? I never touched them."

"Maybe not, but something happened to them."

"Oh, I see. So, you think if you do not touch me, you will be safe? Before, you said…"

"I know what I said," he growled, interrupting her as he pocketed the money. He looked back at her one more time, and she could see the lust and the fear in his eyes. He shook his head, as if trying to dislodge the thoughts and images currently parading through his mind. It was quite clear he was struggling with it, which made her wonder if he could see or smell the primal want coming off her. Finally, with a visible show of effort, the man turned his back on her and jumped back up on the cart. When he snapped the reins to get the horse moving, he did so with a bit too much force, clearly frustrated.

She stood on the porch laughing as she watched the cart leave her yard. When she turned to go back in, she saw Old Boreas standing behind her. He had been inside when she came out, and the door had been closed. She eyed him suspiciously as she reached down to run her fingers over his head.

"How'd you get out, you silly rooster?"

But he seemed to not even hear her. In fact, he also seemed to be watching the cart disappear down the road, as if eyeing the man at the reins. The rooster was deathly still and remained that way until Hannah opened the door to allow them both back inside.

CHAPTER 20

As spring settled in, it did so beautifully. Despite the bitter winter, the warm spring temperatures assisted with the blooming and growth of the trees around the cabin. The smell of flowers she could not even name seemed to always fill her yard, and, to her surprise, there seemed to be little sprouts of grass growing in some places. The yard had always been dead; it had been so inhospitable to grasses that Captain had given up on growing any after the first two years on the property.

The banks of the Wishcaw River were muddy, but the water was flowing nicely. Hannah had been practicing her knots and nets long enough, so when the first truly warm day of spring greeted her, she headed out to put into practice all the things she had learned. She carried two nets she had made herself, as well as a short strand of fishing line, which she figured she could tie from a sapling branch. When she arrived at the river, she kicked over a fallen log and admired the bugs, worms, and other wiggling shapes beneath it. She plucked up three juicy worms and carried them to the edge of the river.

She was quite happy with how easy it all seemed at first, setting her nets according to the instructions in the books she had read. She had a bit of trouble keeping them from floating away but was able to anchor them with stones on the side of the bank and shards of tree branches she stuck into the soft bottom of the relatively shallow water.

With the nets in place, Hannah then tied her line to another branch that she tore from a young tree. It took her awhile to properly hook one of the worms. She pricked herself in the process but considered it something of a payment for her attempts to take life from the river. With the first worm hooked, she took her makeshift fishing pole to the bank and perched herself on a large outcropping of rock.

It took less than three minutes for her to understand why Captain and some of his friends had so enjoyed coming out to the Wishcaw to fish. If she had to guess, it wasn't so much about the actual practice of taking fish from the river but being in the midst of nature. Sitting on the rock with the river gurgling in front of her and the trees swaying in the slight spring breeze behind her, Hannah felt as if she were being purified. She could feel the loneliness and isolation of the winter peeling away and being replaced by some newer, thicker skin—skin that felt almost like armor.

Sunlight filtered through the tree branches, dappling her in odd, fragmented green and yellow light. The voice of the river whispered peaceful gibberish, and even the textured granite on her backside seemed to comfort her. She closed her eyes and let it all sink in—the fresh air, the millions of sounds of the forest all mingling into one, the breeze on her skin...like being embraced and, for just a moment, she allowed herself to think that Old Boreas might be there with her, in the wind and sunlight of the day. Hannah also thought of Captain. She had no idea what happened to the spirit once the flesh rotted, but she thought it entirely possible that it may somehow become part of nature—the wind, the ground, perhaps even the stars in the night sky. *I will be a part of this,* she thought. She sat there with her eyes closed until she felt a sharp tugging sensation in her hands.

She opened her eyes and realized she had held her pole this entire time. In her reverie, she had forgotten. The yank came again, and when she looked out to the water, she could see the small fish breaking the surface as it fought with her line. She had him hooked, that was for sure.

She reached up to the line at the end of her little branch and cupped her fingers around it. She had read that she should softly gather some of it and then pull. Yet, as she started to curl her fingers around the line, the fish pulled hard again, snapping the end of her branch and taking her line into the water with it.

"Shit," she said softly into the beautiful afternoon.

She tossed the remainder of her stick into the water and continued to sit on the rock for quite some time. She looked out to the forest, studying it, losing all track of time as she watched the passage of several deer, countless squirrels, and a writhing black snake making its way through the still-drying foliage and detritus the winter had left behind. Much like herself, she supposed, the snake was on a quest to find a nice rock to warm itself on.

Hannah finally stood up from the stone outcropping when she noticed the light leaving the sky. Her rear end was tingling, and her legs felt cramped. She stretched a bit and walked back through the woods, covering the mile and a half or so it took to get home, thinking she would come back for her nets tomorrow to see what she had caught. According to what she knew there was very little chance she would come up empty-handed unless the nets were washed away, or she had made the netting too large—which she was sure she had not. As she approached the cabin, she noticed Old Boreas sitting on the porch, waiting. He gave Hannah a disappointing cluck when he noticed her hands were empty.

"Take it easy," Hannah said. "It was my first time."

He lowered his head as if he did not want to hear any of it and set about looking for whatever bugs he could dig up from the yard. With the surprising growth of grass, there were plenty of places for them to roam and hide, after all. Hannah left him to his hunt and went inside to make dinner and read up on how she might create a better makeshift pole. She had the money to buy one in town, but figured it was an unnecessary expense. She remembered even Captain had opted for his own pole. He would sit for hours by candlelight making them with an oak limb and basic fishing line. So she figured she could do it as well.

As Hannah was tying the line, she heard something scratch at the door. *Old Boreas*, she thought as she got up from the table and walked toward the door. As she got closer, a slight wind tussled her hair. Light whispers that sounded like buzzing bees filled her ears. She bent slightly, cupping her hands over her ears. She felt her body freeze as the whispers came in like multitudes of fire, burning her ears. *Careful, careful, Hannah*. It was a familiar voice, so deep, yet so soothing. Crisp, almost. A devilish smile lurked at the corners of Hannah's lips as she dropped her arms to her side and turned around. Old Boreas ruffled his feathers, staring at her from the darkened corner of the room. She walked toward him, wondering how he was there. She couldn't remember letting him back in. She was sure when she was working on her fishing pole, Old Boreas was still outside, scrambling about the yard. It reminded her of the day when he was on the porch, staring at the man bringing her firewood.

Hannah moved closer to him. More whispers penetrated the room and bounced off the walls in her cabin. Her brow furrowed as she looked into his eyes. She would have sworn that she saw fire burning within them as she leaned down, scratching his head. Suddenly Old Boreas snapped at her, and Hannah jumped back. She stared curious at the creature as the whispers bellowed again throughout the cabin.

The nights will be warmer now. As the earth warms, so do the hearts of men. And in warmth, there is rot.

She let the words sit in her head for a moment. She studied them. *Rot,* Hannah thought.

"I understand."

The rooster simply looked at her and walked out of the kitchen and into the bedroom. And as Hannah followed close behind, she kept thinking about his eyes, burning through her. And though Old Boreas did not speak again that night, she still heard his voice whispering like the Wishcaw River.

There is rot.

As she laid down to rest that night, there was a fleeting thought that went through her head like a dying stallion across a plain. It felt like a prayer, but she knew better than to talk to the God the folks in Trumbull followed. In fact, she didn't believe in Him at all. She had turned her back on Him years ago. Her prayers went to someone else entirely.

I need answers.

There was, of course, no answer. Just the still and sturdy images that bounced into her mind of a black rooster plucking at her nipples, warm blood dripping down her breast as she lay naked under the moonlight. Millions of stars reflected in the night sky as Hannah pushed the image from her mind and began to smile.

CHAPTER 21

Hannah took a knife and an old pail with her the next day to the river. She stopped by a sturdy-looking oak and stood on her tiptoes to saw at a low-hanging branch. When she was done, she had a rather solid piece of wood, about three feet long and much thicker than her failed pole from the day before.

She checked her nets before casting a new line into the water and was overjoyed to find three fish trapped in one of them. The other net had been swept away by the river, but she didn't really care, she had captured three fish with a net of her own invention. They were all small, one so small she almost tossed it back, but she decided to keep them all and placed them in her pail. Trying the pole again, she tied on a new line, hooked a worm, and cast it out.

With the line in the water, Hannah did the same as the day before. She closed her eyes and relished the feel of nature all around her, breathing it in, letting it consume her. She listened to every sound: the wind through the trees, some small animal moving not too far away, the birdsong, a croaking toad, the rushing water, the insects, all of it. It all seemed to speak to her in the same way Old Boreas spoke to her, only it was quieter and much less striking. There were whispers, and in those whispers, there were shapes of words that she could not make out. But it was all encouraging. Some of it even felt loving.

The day ended without any curious fish taking her bait. She kept the rod, wrapping the line around it and carrying it back to the cabin under her arm, along with the three captured fish in the pail. As she made her way home, she felt as if she were floating. She had managed to catch fish, and the last two days out in open nature seemed to have washed through her in a way that made no sense. She was thinking more clearly, feeling more alive than she had since Captain had been killed.

She was so caught up in this feeling of elation that she did not see the snakes on her porch until she had raised her foot to step on it. She only saw four at first, but then she noticed two longer ones near her door. They were all black, except for one of the longer ones. She was quite certain that one was a copperhead.

By the time she realized there were seven in all, she saw something else on the porch. Nestled between two of the snakes was the crushed body of a rabbit. There was a second hare in the corner of the porch, looking at her with its small, dead eyes as one of the black snakes coiled up protectively at its side.

The snakes clearly knew she was there. Those that had been coiled up loosened and slithered to their full length, and though it both looked and seemed impossible, she was quite sure they were making a path for her. Some of the snakes went to one side of the porch while the rest slithered to the other, leaving a thin aisle between them that led directly to her front door, with the first dead rabbit sitting in the center of this little path.

A fluttering noise to her right tore her eyes away from the snakes and their grisly gifts. It was Old Boreas making his way to the porch, which calmed her a bit. When she watched him hop up onto the porch and make his way down the pathway between the snakes, she was even more relieved. Some deep part of her knew she should have questioned what was before her, but it was quickly overruled by the strange beauty of how the snakes once again had parted for her.

Old Boreas stopped when he came to the rabbit. He looked back to her and said: *Come. Food. Meat.*

Hannah finally placed her still-raised foot onto the porch, but none of the snakes moved at all. In fact, they seemed to regard her with an odd sort of respect—the same way some well-trained dogs tended to heel for their masters. She bent down for the first rabbit and carefully stepped among the snakes to get the second. She wanted to fear them, relying on an old fear of serpents, but there was nothing like that. In fact, as she picked up the limp bodies of the rabbits, she felt a sense of gratitude. It was much like what she had felt when she'd closed her eyes at the river, letting the beauty of nature sink into her skin.

With the dead rabbits in one hand and her pail of fish in the other, Hannah entered the cabin. When she held the door open for Old Boreas, she looked at the serpents on the porch for a moment. Feeling curious, she tilted her head the way Old Boreas often did and said: "Come inside."

Three of the black snakes instantly moved. To her delight, they came inside the cabin, one right after the other, passing through the doorway slowly, with reverence. The remaining four, however, made their way off the porch, slithering in an eerie sort of unison.

Hannah gave one final glance to her new visitors before closing the door. Then, with a smile on her face that felt ghostly, she said, "Welcome home."

CHAPTER 22

The next day, as she made her way to what she now thought of as her "fishing rock," she was aggravated to see that someone else was already there. She knew her irritation was foolish; it was open land, and the forest belonged to no one. Many men used the Wishcaw River for fishing, and this little haven she had found could be used by anyone. Still, she wanted to place her nets back into the river. She had eaten well the night before, even though she had butchered some of the rabbit meat by skinning them improperly. And though the rabbit had been filling, she could still taste the cooked fish and it made her mouth water.

As she drew closer, she took a swift side glance to get a better look at the fisherman. To her surprise, he wasn't a fisherman at all. It was a young man who seemed to be no older than sixteen. He turned quickly as she drew closer and, for a moment, she thought he was going to drop his pole and run—her appearance had been so sudden.

"You-you startled me," the boy said, embarrassed. He eyed her for a moment, and the look of bewilderment that came across his face told Hannah all she needed to know. He was acutely aware of who she was.

"Did I?" Hannah said, moving closer. "I did not mean to, but I'd like to put my nets in here. I've been practicing, you see, and I seem to have had some luck in this spot."

The boy thought about this for a while, then nodded. He started to quickly draw his line out of the water, quickly looking back and forth from the river, and back to Hannah.

"You can have the spot," he said. "I'll move farther down."

"There is no need for that," Hannah said, smiling, rather enjoying the odd look on his face. She saw the fright easily enough, but there was a light reddening to his cheeks as well. His eyes were large and expressive and, as she looked into them, Hannah took another step forward. She could hear the announcements of the forest already, even though she was not perched on her rock, willing the noises to come. The forest seemed to be anxious, as if it were expecting something, and even though she still couldn't understand its language, the urging tones reminded her of Old Boreas yet again.

"It's OK," the boy said. "I don't mind."

"So, tell me, are you a good fisherman?" Hannah asked.

The boy shrugged. "I guess." The posture of the shrug and the creaking of his voice told Hannah even more. He *was* scared, but his curiosity was winning out. She thought of the children from the woods and the Constable who had come by her house. She thought of Old Boreas and the snakes. Most of all, she thought of Captain falling into the mouth of Wayman's Gorge. She smiled at the memories but held the boy's gaze. She was very aware of what he was doing. His eyes slid down her body, pausing at the hips where her dress sculpted her shape, then at her breasts where her cleavage was screaming to be touched.

"I'm having the hardest time getting anything to bite when I throw a line in," she said. "Do you think you could show me what I'm doing wrong?" The conflict on his face was adorable. Hannah was not particularly proud of it, but she found herself aroused by his confused expression.

She felt the fear coming from him. For Hannah, it was like a drug that made her scream for more. She wanted to satisfy that hunger. She knew it was because of who she was and because he was in the forest, isolated and alone with her. The power she had over him was intoxicating, and she wanted more right away.

"I really shouldn't," he said.

"What's your name?"

"Thomas. Thomas Dunne."

Hannah raised her brow. The forest whispered again, and

this time, the sound came in like a flood, roaring through the trees like a gust of wind. *Dunne*, she thought.

"Well, Thomas...Thomas Dunne, you need not be afraid of me. No matter what you may have heard, you can trust me. Do I *look* frightening, Thomas?"

He was still shaking his head, but his eyes never left hers. One hand was still on the line at the end of his rod, but he was no longer pulling it in. He was staring at her, transfixed.

"Are you Pastor Dunne's son?"

He nodded. "No, ma'am. That's my grandpa."

Hannah laughed. "I'm not a ma'am. Can you tell me some of the things you've heard from your grandpa about me?" She took two steps closer to him, coming to the edge of the rock, and he barely seemed to notice. If she wanted to, she could reach out and touch him.

"He says you're with the devil, that you killed your husband. Yeah, you made a deal with the devil."

"And yet, here I am, living alone and having to spring fish from the river. What the hell sort of deal does people think I made?"

With his eyes still locked on her, Thomas was trembling and slowly easing away. His eyes widened, and his lips were quivering slightly. "They say you're a witch."

"Do you believe that?" she asked. "That I am a witch?"

Thomas opened his mouth to speak, but nothing escaped. The ground shifted and the air grew thin as voices escaped from the earth like rumbling thunder. Thomas blinked rapidly and looked all around him.

"What are you doing?" he asked timidly, speaking like a child who had been yanked out of a dream. "What are you trying to do to me?" The murmuring sounds around them grew louder.

"I'm not doing anything, Thomas."

"You *are* a witch!"

She smiled again and took another step toward him. Thomas tried to take a step back, but he could not move. His body froze, and his flesh went cold.

"Maybe I am," she said. She reached up slowly and undid two of the buttons at the neck of her dress. As the second one sprang open, the delicate valley between her breasts were revealed. "But do you think I look like a witch, Thomas?"

He said nothing, but his eyes took in the new sight she had given him. While he was distracted, Hannah reached out and took his hand. "Thomas," she repeated, interlocking her fingers in his, "do I look like a witch?"

His mouth hung open, but no words came out. He dropped his fishing rod and did not notice when it clattered to the ground. She saw the lust in his eyes like some huge and awakening dragon. Sixteen or not, he was very much a man in that moment. And even though Hannah continued to eye Thomas in a lustful fashion, the slogan of the winter swirled through her head.

Let them fear you...

Using her free hand to pluck two more buttons loose, she drew him closer when her breasts were completely exposed. "Would you like to touch them? No one needs to know."

Thomas stuttered. Hannah raised one thin finger and caressed her neck, drawing a line between her breasts before grabbing his hand. She placed it on her exposed nipples, urging him to caress her. He did as she wished, and Hannah sighed. The sound urged him to step closer. He ran his thumb along the underside, then up across her other nipple.

"Oh, yes," he said. His voice was flat and dry and sounded nothing like the voice he had been speaking with only moments before. His fear was now gone, and he was thinking only of the softness of Hannah's touch.

"Have you ever been with a woman before?" she asked, watching as he began to stroke his penis.

"No. Momma said it's a sin. It's the devil's work."

"Oh, you poor boy," she said as she drew him closer. She took his other hand and placed it on her hips, and he clung to her at once, trembling.

"It's OK, Thomas. I promise," Hannah whispered as she unbuttoned the rest of her dress. It slid to the ground, and she stepped out of it. She stood nude in front of him, free, and she was unsure what she enjoyed more—the look of absolute hunger in the boy's eyes, or the feeling of the open, fresh air on her body. Hannah felt as though there were a million hands slowly caressing her skin, accepting her into the grips of the earth.

Stupefied by what he saw before him, Thomas dropped his hands away from her hip and breast. For a moment, he seemed to be paralyzed.

"Touch me, Thomas," Hannah whispered.

"Where?" he asked, his face redder than ever, but now there was a delicate confidence to him as he eased closer to her. Even with his inexperience revealed in that one-word question, he seemed oddly certain of himself.

"Wherever you'd like."

An image of the man who delivered her stove wood ran through her mind, and she felt every nerve in her body wanting this more. Then the banker's words echoed in her mind.

"Well, Mrs. Hovey, you are a woman. You are not allowed to own property. So, Mr. Hovey, concerned about you, set up a stipulation." And her desire peaked even more. But there was also something else beneath the simple carnal desires and need for revenge. There was something dark and delicious that she could not name.

With an inexperienced caution, Thomas started at her breasts, touching the right one again as if he were afraid it would break, trailing his fingers down her navel to the thatch of hair between her legs. Hannah could not help the moan that escaped her lips, nor could she contain the trembling that tore through her. Thomas drew away at first, but when he understood that the sound, she'd made had been one of pleasure, he was right back to the task. He cupped her there and she leaned into him, grinding gently against him as his finger fumbled for entrance.

Hannah reached down and guided him. She gasped when one of his fingers slid into her and cried out when a second followed. She reached out to grab him by the shirt, to lead him to the rock and have him take her, but again, his free hand found another purpose. He took her hand and guided it to his pants. She felt him beneath the fabric, so hard it could have been a rock hiding in his trousers. She gripped the shape of him and slid her hand slowly back and forth. She started fumbling for the button, but just as he began to truly explore her, the wind gusted rapidly, and the whispers of laughter filled his ears. The forest was alive again all around them, and Thomas began to choke. He quickly withdrew his fingers and jumped back as if Hannah had bitten him. Hannah's hand was suddenly empty. The lust and desire were gone from his face. They were replaced by a look of horror and shame.

"What did...?" he said.

Hannah began to laugh as she felt her own desires and wishes fleeing from her. She made a snapping noise with her tongue and watched as Thomas shook his head and broke into a series of spasms. He tried to scream, but it came out in a choked noise, almost like a dog's bark. His eyes rolled upward, and he fell hard to the ground, right beside his fishing pole.

Hannah stood over him for a moment, taking it all in. She looked down at the unconscious boy and, with a devilish smile parting her lips, she leaned down and kissed him.

"So sorry, Thomas," she said, pushing his golden hair back from his forehead. But even as she pulled her dress back up and started walking back home, she was not quite sure what it was that she was sorry for.

CHAPTER 23

That night, she dreamed that Thomas had violently taken her from behind on the rock. She cried out in pleasure with every thrust and climaxed so many times that she lost count, but as he worked on her, hundreds of snakes started to come out of the forest. They came from under tree roots, from the river, and from soggy patches of moss and mud. Some fell from the trees and slithered around the young man's back. They bit him and choked him, but he went on and on, slamming so hard into her that she thought her pelvis would break. She placed her face against the rock, with each hard thrust, her cheek was ripped open by the granite. As the warm blood flowed from her face, Hannah screamed with pleasure.

She saw a single black snake crawl on the rock in front of

her. Its eyes locked on her and, with a little hiss, it repeated the words from Old Boreas.

As the earth warms, so do the hearts of men. And in warmth, there is rot.

As the snake wrapped around her arm, Hannah woke up, sitting up slowly as the early morning light crept in through the window. She looked over to the kitchen and saw two of the snakes she had invited in two days ago. One was curled tightly and resting, and the other was slithering about and exploring the space beneath the wood stove. As for Old Boreas, he was perched on the end of her bed as usual. He looked at her with his routine sense of wonder and care, and something about the idea of him watching her while she slept made her feel desired.

As she got up from her bed, she knew it was time to start her day. She had a small breakfast before getting dressed. She noticed that, as she moved around the cabin, the snakes seemed to keep away from her. It occurred to her that perhaps they could sense her loyalty and were respecting her, keeping their distance. After the dream she'd had, she greatly appreciated the gesture.

After several hours of doing nothing, Hannah thought of Thomas until she became restless and wondered about the big world out there again. Old Boreas jumped and gawked at her. That was his way of wishing her thoughts away.

"I know, Old Boreas, there's nothing for me out there. You

crazy rooster," Hannah said to him, ruffling his head. But still, it was a special sort of hell to sit around the cabin all day, with a rooster—and now snakes—for her only company. She had read every book in the house since Captain had died (some two or three times) and while she could stand to work on her fishing skills a bit more, the previous day's events had her wondering if she should venture back out to the river so soon.

She was fine admitting she had liked the boy's touch, but the feeling of being one with nature was what she really enjoyed. Thomas was just a bonus for her, and something she had to do. Even then, sitting at the table and thinking of the boy's eyes devouring her, Hannah felt an immense satisfaction in what she had done.

She got up from the table and took stock of what was in the pantry. She wouldn't need to head into town for groceries anytime soon, but she liked to know what sort of meals she could plan for. She had enough flour to last awhile, but she could use some eggs. Similarly, there were plenty of oats and a good amount of jerky remaining. She would need salt before too long, and she would really like to get some fresh fruit, which had always been difficult to come by in Trumbull.

Thinking of fruit, her mind somehow conjured up an image of Emma Nichols and her amazing pies. The mere thought of cutting into one of those pies made her mouth water. Between her mouth and her womanhood, Hannah thought she might be feeling just a little too needy today.

Figuring there would be no harm in at least trying, she took a bit of money from the candy tin and placed it in one of the little pockets in the black dress she was wearing. When she turned to the door to leave, Old Boreas stood there as if he planned to escort her. When she opened the door, the snakes came slithering to her as well. The snakes went out first, perhaps seeking the comfort of the sun. Old Boreas went next, followed by Hannah. The snakes made their way down the porch and went their separate ways, while the black rooster remained by Hannah's side until they came to the edge of the yard. There, Old Boreas stopped and watched her start down the road.

Hannah knew he was her protector of sorts. He had never left the property ever since she had allowed him inside. The closest he had ever come was strutting about the edge of the tree line to keep some of the bothersome kids away and warning her of what is to come.

And what else is coming? she wondered.

She had nearly forgotten the dark object that had moved out there among the trees to chase the meddling children away. But now, as she recalled it, the idea of it was more than enough to cause her to look out into the forest, now speckled with fresh spring colors, and remember it. She did not fear it, of course she didn't, but she was also not eager to see it again—whatever it might have been. She thought it might be like some disillusioned sea captain: aware of the leviathans that lurked below him but casting them out of his mind in an effort to keep madness away. That's what Hannah thought it was. Maybe that's what she was.

She made her way to the Nichols property. She was so preoccupied with her thoughts that she found herself standing in front of their house without any real recollection of walking there. She could hear at least one of the girls running around behind the house, laughing and singing. As for Emma Nichols, she was sitting on the front porch with one bowl in her lap and another sitting between her feet. It appeared that she was shelling peas. Hannah stared across the yard, vastly aware of the two conflicting moods swirling through her. Part of her wanted to be the scary, brooding witch everyone in Trumbull thought her to be, but another part of her still wanted to try to get Emma Nichols on her good side. That's what Old Boreas told her, anyway. Even to Hannah, Emma seemed like a kind enough spirit who just needed guidance and to be swayed away from this so-called God she had put all her faith in. Emma had given Hannah some mean looks and cross words but had never been out-and-out cruel to her. Plus, Hannah knew Emma was keeping a secret, a dirty little secret, and Hannah figured she was just the person to bring it to the surface.

Hannah was roughly halfway across the lawn when Emma noticed her. The two women simply stared at one another for a moment before Emma got to her feet and came to the edge of the porch, still carrying her bowl of shelled peas.

"Hannah," Emma said. "Wh-what can I do for you? Do you remember what Rube told you about coming here?"

"I do, but—"

"No buts. It's not safe for you here. You know that."

"Not safe?" Hannah laughed at such a gesture. "Well, maybe we can meet in the woods again, Emma? We will be *safe* there." Hannah raised her brow and smiled.

Emma took a step back, widening her eyes. Hannah was pretty sure she could see the bowl trembling in her grasp.

"No, why would I do such a thing? I am a God-fearing woman, Hannah Crannah, and don't you go about spreading lies about me! You hear me?"

The anger in her voice was layered with fear, but Hannah was shocked by the abrupt nature of it. In response, something rose in her, lifting its head like a serpent about to strike.

"Emma, you're a smart woman. Surely you can understand that all things are never what they seem. Can't you?"

"What I *understand* is that every piece of produce I have cut into since giving you that pie during the winter has been rotten. Anything I cut into or pluck, it doesn't matter. It's all nice and ripe when I get it home. But the moment I cut into them—they spoil. They rot right before my eyes, full of bugs and worms like they've crawled out from the mouth of the beast! You cursed me, Hannah! You cursed me! Made me feel of rot. And if Rube finds out, he will come for you and bring the wrath of God with him."

"Oh yes, wraths' of God and the rots of men. Ironic, isn't it?" Hannah smiled and took a step forward, pointing to Emma's face. "I see your husband already took that wrath out on you, huh?" Emma raised her hand to her cheek.

"That doesn't matter. I am just saying he will handle it in his own way. That's all. I heard about the children in the woods. The church is in an uproar about it and you. Rube is there now. I guess they're discussing what to do about you. I am just saying, it's not safe for you here, not anymore."

Hannah said nothing. She only nodded. A thin smile came to her lips, and it felt natural. That dark thing that had started to raise its head growled inside of her. Much like the way the spring-soaked forest seemed to sink into her and fill her, this presence did the same thing. She could feel it behind her eyes, tingling at her fingertips, coating her brain in something like fuzz.

"So be it," Hannah said.

She was quite certain it was not her voice that came out of her throat when she spoke those three words. As she turned around and left the woman's yard, she was quite certain she could hear some useless, silly prayer pouring from Emma's mouth. Though Hannah paid very little attention to the prayer, she could not ignore how each word felt like a little dagger of fire striking her in the back and stinging her skin. *They will see*, she thought as she walked back to her cabin and saw Old Boreas waiting for her on the tree line of her property. Her little hero, always watching and waiting to strike. Hannah smiled and began humming. It was a song she was not familiar with, but it seemed so peaceful and relaxing.

CHAPTER 24

Spring played itself out with fresh crops and blooms in the town of Trumbull. The trees were filled with foliage, and the skies were usually clear aside from a brief pelting of rain. It was a spring where corn was brought in from neighboring counties and traded to Trumbull locals for things like hay and fish—even though Hannah was not particularly skilled at taking fish out of the river, there were spots along the Wishcaw where expert fisherman could easily pull trout and catfish consistently.

It was a spring that saw the unfortunate death of the local grocer, who had not so long before feared Hannah but continued to do business with her any way. Based on the whispers Hannah picked up around town, he died of heart failure, but Hannah knew better. He had been buried on a

Thursday morning. Twenty-two people showed up for his funeral, though that was a sizable number for a funeral in Trumbull.

On that very same morning, Hannah was sitting on her front porch with three snakes coiled up beside her while Old Boreas was off in the yard pecking around for worms or beetles. Hannah had not left her home since her conversation with Emma Nichols and since Pastor Dunne and the Constable had informed her that she was not allowed in town until they got things sorted out about the children. Mary O'Keeffe had succumbed to her disease, and the other boys had been moved to a small medical ward in Virginia. She had known nothing of the passing of the girl, but she heard something on the light breeze a few days later, something like wailing and gnashing, something that felt like grief in the air, jabbing again and again. It smelled like rot.

She figured it was grief, but she did not know where it came from. She closed her eyes and tilted her head slightly. The sadness was in the air. There had been a great loss in Trumbull.

"What's happened, Old Boreas?"

The rooster stopped its hunting and seemed to look out toward the path that led into the town. He looked at Hannah as if he were angry that she had disrupted his hunting with such trivial matters. Then he went back to pecking and kicking up dirt.

Hannah did not learn of the grocer's passing until she ventured into town four days later. Even then, she went only out of necessity. She was out of flour and, as of late, had started to develop a taste for sweets. Dismissing the Constable's warning, she jotted down her brief list, gathered up enough money to pay for it all, and headed into town.

Despite the spring's growing heat, she still wore her cloak. With the hood partially over her long hair, Hannah thought it made the walk into town warmer than she liked. When she arrived in Trumbull, she was sweating lightly, and she felt disheveled. Turning the corner to go to the grocer's shop, she hesitated at the sight of her reflection in the murky window along the side of the porch.

She studied her features for a moment. The reflection in the glass made her look ghostlike, but that was not what struck her. What really grabbed her attention was how beautiful she looked. It was not a conceited notion. She did not stand there to appreciate how good she looked, but to try to understand what had happened to her. Captain, on his kind days, had always made a point to let her know how beautiful she was and had told her stories about how he had thrown a punch or two at some of the men he had encountered when they made remarks about her appearance. Hannah had never truly believed him, though she did appreciate the compliments and the way he always did his best to make her feel wanted. *Wanted, huh? Too much*, she thought as she remembered the last time she'd felt his hand strike her cheek. "Never again." The whispers blew against a brief gust of wind in her ear.

Hannah pushed the hood away from her face. Her eyes widened as she stared at her reflection and stroked her cheeks. She supposed she could see it—but it was not like looking at herself. The slim figure hugged by the black dress under her cloak, the slightly messy hair barely falling along the side of her face, the full lips, the perfect curve of her breasts...and behind it all, almost like some sort of body-shaped halo, she saw something else. Not a glow—but maybe the opposite of it. It looked almost like a shadow radiating off her, but that wasn't quite right, either. It was if someone was attached to her, their own figure barely showing off her own. And as she studied it, she watched it breathe and bend. It was radiating and—

"What're you doing there, witch?"

The voice, tight and snappy, pulled her away from her reflection. She smiled and turned toward the voice. It was a small man coming out of the grocer's shop. He was pudgy around the waist and old around the eyes and had a hardened red tinge around his nose and mouth that often came with excessive drinking of moonshine and liquor. She could even see it in his eyes, reddened right along the corners.

"I'm doing nothing," she said. "Just a bit of shopping." She hesitated for a moment, eyeing the man. "What business is it of yours?"

"It's every damned bit my business," the man said. "This is my store now, in case you didn't know."

Confused, Hannah looked around at anyone who might be in the street. There were only a few people milling about, and only one was watching her—an elderly lady with wide eyes, trembling slightly.

"Well, isn't that a hankering," Hannah said sarcastically. "And the other man?"

"He died. Buried just a few days ago. Now, I understand it that he would allow you to shop here, but I'm not going to show you such grace. I know what you are, Hannah... Hannah Crannah! Your money is no good here."

"Ahhh yes. I could have sworn I smelled him rot. But I was not sure."

"Blasphemy toward the dead. You are vile woman! Aye, and your presence is an affront to God Almighty, and I'll not have you darkening the doorsteps of any business I'm running."

Fury and a writhing darkness boiled up inside her, but she managed to keep it down. "Blasphemy, blasphemy. Always Blasphemy. But it's a small town, sir. Wherever will I get my food?" Hannah said, smiling as she stepped forward. The man stepped back, but Hannah did not sense as much fear from him as she did others.

"That's not my issue," the man said. "Now, because I *am* a godly man, and you seem not to have known about the previous owner, I'll grant you one trip into my store...right now. You stock up on all you need, but I don't want to see you around here again. Do you understand that?"

"Of course," Hannah said, feeling that darkness stretching out and wanting to lash out. She recalled the feeling of absolute power she had held over Thomas for that brief period and yearned for it as she stood in front of this man. She wanted it to come out like a thief but also knew that in that moment, it might not be a good idea.

"You get on in there and do your business. You have ten minutes, and then I want you out, or I will call the preacher and the Constable. Rumor has it, you have been banished from town and should not be here in the first place. So go on, hurry up."

Hannah nodded and walked slowly to the door of the store. There was something inside of her that insisted she should not worry about this—something fiendish. And she was far too angry to care about such things. In fact, the anger took over and etched a smile across her face as she started gathering up food items, some of which she didn't even need. She was very aware of the grocer watching her. He had gone back behind the counter and taken out a well-worn Bible, his hands resting on top of it as he eyed her making her way through the aisles.

She brought the flour to the counter last. The grocer tallied everything as quickly as he could, not bothering to even look at her. When he was done and gave her the total, Hannah eyed the man curiously.

"This is quite a lot, you know. I'll have to make two trips. That is…unless you have someone who can help take it for me."

"Two trips are fine," he said. "What you can't take now, I'll leave on the back stoop."

She nodded curtly and tossed her money down on the counter. As he reached for it, she quickly placed her hand over his other hand, which was still resting on his Bible. She smiled, and he stepped back. His eyes widened and his cheeks turned pale as his rage turned into fear. Hannah pushed herself forward, then hefted the bag of flour up on her shoulder. A light film of white dust and powder streaked her black dress. The man jumped back in fear. Sweat beaded his forehead as he made a religious motion across his chest.

Hannah smiled again and raised her brows. "This God of yours…would He be as cruel as you are? Having me carry these groceries half a mile down the road alone? Banishing me from a town with no worry to others? Or maybe He would be too preoccupied with turning women into pillars of salt and waiting for the next dead goat to be delivered to His heavenly door?"

The look of horror that spread across his face drew a small chuckle from Hannah's throat. As she exited the store, lugging the sack of flour and a small sack of groceries, she could hear Old Boreas whispering to her, *"There are no devils."* But Hannah wasn't so sure about that. She figured they just came from places that most people worshipped as saints. Like angels with devil wings.

Standing on the porch, she noticed more people gathered outside in the streets watching her, moving their lips in secret like bored sows waiting to be slaughtered. The Constable emerged from the crowd holding a stick. Hannah smiled at him as she adjusted the flour, held her head high and walked toward Crow Trail. The flour was heavy, but she made sure to not let the people in Trumbull see her struggle. She grunted to herself and began to sweat all over again. As Hannah walked past the church, a thin voice stopped her in her tracks.

"Gee, lady, you need a hand with that?"

Hannah turned and saw a young boy, surely no older than ten years of age, standing on the side of the road. Carrying a stick that had been fashioned into a crude little spear, he had the pelts of two dead animals draped over his shoulder.

Hannah looked down at him. "Why? Do you want to carry it?"

"Oh, yeah. I've got muscles. See, momma says so."

Hannah considered this for a moment and nodded. "Do you know who I am?"

"They say you're a witch. Are you?"

"Maybe? What if I am?"

The boy grinned and shook his head. "You fly around? You kill little kids for their blood? Things like that?"

"No. Not yet anyway," Hannah giggled.

"You got a cat that follows you everywhere?" the boy asked.

"No, I don't have a cat. I do have a rooster, though. Maybe you could meet him. Now, are you sure you want to help me?"

"Yeah, I'm sure. Momma always says God's children should help people in need—women, elderly, and something-minded folks. I can't think of the word."

"I see. Well, here you go, young man," she said, lowering the flour to him. He took it and carried it in front of him, as his shoulders weren't quite large enough to support the sack.

"See, it's not that heavy," he said, though he grunted with each word.

"Good. Now, my house is the last one on this road, right where it ends. You go ahead and walk, and I'll catch up to you. I've got more groceries back at the shop."

"Alright, ma'am."

She watched as the boy walked forward, clearly straining from the weight, but getting accustomed to it. Hannah smiled at him and turned to walk back to the grocer's, hoping the crowd had dispersed. Before she could get in a few steps toward the town, she saw two people looking at her from the porch of the church, both aghast and afraid. One was a middle-aged man, staring at her as if she had beaten the boy who had helped her. The other was a frail old woman sweeping the steps and cursing at what she had seen.

"You'll be damned for that," the old woman yelled. "The boy, too, I reckon. God will not forgive."

Hannah walked slowly to the edge of the grass, cocked her head, staring so intently her eyes began to bulge. "None of us are damned, ma'am. Don't you know...there are no devils."

She felt the woman and then the man pressing their eyes back to her with complete disgust. The door of the church opened, and Pastor Dunne walked to the edge of the porch, never taking his eyes off her. His black trousers were held up with white suspenders, his face looked frail, and Hannah could smell the disease protruding from his eyes.

Suddenly, the air shifted as a gust of wind twirled behind her. Whispers in her mind buzzed like wasps, batting and stinging her in multiple ways. *Treasures gained by wickedness shall not profit. You shall purge the evil from your midst.*

"Burn!" Hannah screamed as the wind whipped through her hair. She closed her eyes and lifted her hands as the earth shook beneath her. When she opened her eyes again, she saw Pastor Dunne scurrying back into the church, slamming the door behind him.

Hannah had no idea what the comment meant, but it came to her quickly, like rolling summer thunder off her tongue. The old woman gasped, and Hannah devoured her fear as she turned and walked back to the grocer's.

CHAPTER 25

Hannah fully expected to catch up with the young boy on her way to her cabin. Surely, he would not have reached her property lugging that sack of flour so quickly. But when she got home, she was surprised to see that he had. She noticed the flour on her porch, near the bottom step, then heard screams coming from the side of her house. She hurried around the cabin and found him near the barn flanked by two older boys. She assumed they had come out of the woods after him. They looked to be older, maybe fifteen or so, and their skin was caked with dirt and sweat. They were taunting the boy, pressing him against the barn and laughing. She wasn't sure, but she thought she recognized the face of one of the older boys—perhaps he had been one of the adventurous chaps that had urinated in her yard the morning Pastor Dunne had come by to pick up Captain's belongings.

"She pay you for lugging her crap?" the bigger boy asked.

"Yeah," said the other, poking him in the chest. "How's she paying you? Did she let you see her naked?"

"Did she put your pecker in her mouth?"

The two older boys broke into riotous laughter but neither of them noticed that Hannah was slowly crossing the yard with two sacks of groceries. They didn't hear her until she put the sacks on the ground a few feet away from them. They wheeled around quickly. Hannah noticed the smaller of the two looked like he was about to take off running, while the other stared at Hannah, alarmed and frightful.

"What are you doing back here?" Hannah yelled, flailing her hand toward them.

"Stay away from me, witch!" the older boy said. Cold fear seemed to have invaded his body. Hannah saw it deep in his eyes and heard it in his voice. "You stay away from me, or I'll tell…I'll tell my father!"

"Your father," Hannah laughed. "Your father is a worm from the earth's dust. I do not fear your father. Why would I? But maybe you should tell him you are trespassing on my land, you little brute, and threatening my guest!"

"He won't believe you if you tell him that. He don't seek the devil."

Hannah took a step closer to the three boys. The one

who had carried the flour looked almost amused. The others seemed desperate to do anything not to stare into her eyes.

A warm gust of wind came whooshing by her, and she felt the darkness awake inside of her. Something slithered by her feet, and she smiled, tilting her head toward the children. It was her snakes. They had never spoken to her like Old Boreas did, but she could *feel* their presence and their power as they passed by her. It felt like something boiling inside of her and on the verge of exploding, like gunpowder inches away from a flame, a coiling sort of threat confined to their serpentine bodies. The wind picked up again when a third snake followed them. This was the copperhead that had been sticking around and making itself known.

"I won't bother telling him," Hannah said. Her stare never wavered. "You will. You'll tell your father how you were threatening what is looking to be the only kindhearted soul in this filthy town. You'll tell him, and then you'll pray to your dirty preacher for forgiveness. Isn't that how it works? You little ratbags! You run around here doing what you please and then go to church on Sunday? Isn't it?"

"You crazy witch!" the boy screamed, mostly to mask the fear that was tearing through him. Hannah watched as his body tensed and shook. She could *smell* it. It was a sweet smell, though there was an underlying sort of musk to it, almost like mottled moss. She had a craving for it, a hunger she could not control.

"Sammy, shut your mouth," the smaller one whispered.

"Oh, I'll tell my father you tried to curse me! I'll tell him that you—"

His eyes widened again as he noticed the snakes coming out of nowhere. They had slithered near him and flanked him against the barn. The two black snakes parted to allow the copperhead in the middle, its brown and gold scales glistening like oil. It slithered closer, then hovered in place.

"Call them off!" the boy hollered. "You call them off!"

"I didn't call them at all," Hannah said, "you did." She could sense the boys' terror and wanted to scream with laughter. "You called them. You called them when you came here on my land."

"I'll tell! I'll tell and—"

One snake leaped into the air. It was not a straight line of slithering blackness darting forward like an arrow, but more like some strange dark sinew blowing on the wind. She had heard Captain tell stories about seeing black snakes give chase to those who threatened them. She had even heard him describe one snake that stood on its tail and somehow pushed itself along to move faster.

The snake draped itself over the boy's shoulder and clamped its jaws into the back of his neck. Once its teeth were in, it curled itself around it. The boy howled and fell to the ground, his head striking the side of the cabin as he tried to pull the snake away. The other black snake launched itself in the same way toward the second boy, though this one did not quite reach the height of its kin. It struck the smaller boy's leg but, before it fell to the ground, it bit hard along the boy's knee. He was wearing a pair of thick trousers, but Hannah could tell that the snake's fangs tore through them easily, dangling there for a moment before releasing and nipping at the boy's ankles.

The boy went running right away, speeding off into the trees with the snake dangling from his leg. She could see it not just sinking its fangs in, but continuously biting. The boy was crying and shrieking, his cries filtering through the forest. Meanwhile, his friend remained in Hannah's yard. He tried to get to his feet to run but was too distracted by the snake that continued to bite and bite and bite, now tearing into the meat of his shoulder. It had drawn blood, which was trickling down the boy's dirty skin.

The copperhead watched. Hannah could tell it was simply waiting, ready to spring out just like the other two, and she also knew that a copperhead bite could be fatal.

She slowly tilted her head. It felt like an act of obedience, and it caused that dark rage inside of her to shift. Her stomach felt uneasy, and her head started to ache and ring. Hannah popped a sound with her tongue and the copperhead drafted forward, striking out with lethal accuracy and speed. It caught the boy in the back of the leg, sinking its fangs into the meat and drawing blood instantly. Hannah watched it drip down his legs. It was so slight, so harmless, but she knew the truth of it.

The copperhead released almost at once and stared up at Hannah before it slithered away through the grass, back to the forest that surrounded her house. The larger boy was howling now, sounding more like a wounded dog than a terrified scoundrel. He cast one last look back over his shoulder as he fell to his knees while escaping through the woods. He wheezed in terror, tried to open his mouth to scream but couldn't. He struggled to his feet and entered the forest, trying to get to safety.

Hannah stood there watching, smiling, and loving the sight of it.

Please...there's no return from this, she thought, and quickly got a response. It came from behind her in a deep, familiar voice.

Why would you want to return?

Hannah turned and smiled as she saw Old Boreas standing behind her. He looked intensely at her, even when the third boy started slinking away. He walked quickly to the road, not daring to take his eyes off her. There were still little white streaks of dust on his forearms from where he had carried her flour.

"Thanks for your help," she yelled. "I didn't mean to—"

Ah, but didn't you? Old Boreas interrupted her.

The boy was weeping, wiping tears from his face as he

finally broke into a run. He ran down the road back into town, and Hannah could only imagine what sort of news he would deliver to the folks of Trumbull—people who were so vile that Hannah didn't care for them in the first place.

She sighed for a moment, then turned back to Old Boreas. Out of the corner of her right eye, she could see the black snakes making their escape to the back of the barn.

"What have I done? What have I become? What sort of...*devil* am I?"

She heard laughter in her head, thick and sludge like. It made her think of swamps and molasses.

You daft woman, Old Boreas said. *Didn't you know? There are no devils.*

CHAPTER 26

You give me your hands, Hannah. You just give them here and this will be over before you know it. This is for your own good. The Good Lord loves us all, even the worst of the whores, but there must be a punishment. There is always a punishment of evil, Hannah. Now give me your hands, the ones you touched yourself with. Are you a whore, Hannah?"

Hannah knew it was a dream. Only in dreams did she see her mother's face clearly. Her waking mind had long ago distorted the images, but her sleeping memories kept it fresh and always at the ready. She knew it was a dream, but that didn't mean she feared the stump and the hammer any less.

She placed her small hands on the old stump just a few yards behind the encampment border. She saw her mother lift the hammer, but never thought she would use it. Maybe this was just a threat, maybe just a pretend thing where she—

The right hand was first. The hammer came down, and somehow, the crunch was as loud as the gunshots she often heard coming from the south in the afternoons. The pain was like nothing she had ever experienced before, a swirling, spiked heat that tore through her and made her heart feel as if it had shriveled in her chest. At eight years old, Hannah drew in a breath to scream, but before she could let it out, the left hand caught the same punishment.

In the dream, Hannah's scream came out sounding like the babbling of the creek behind the house—the creek she had not yet learned to properly fish from. The scream served as the end of the dream, but as her eyes shot open like a gun, Hannah remembered it all. As she lay in the silence of her cabin, she recalled her mother's touch as she had drawn her to her bosom and hugged her. She also remembered her own screams and how she had held her broken hands to her chest, wailing and thrashing.

"'Tis for your own good," her mother had said. "Hannah, if I catch you touching yourself again, we may have to have the doctor man make it so that it doesn't feel good anymore. I don't want to...but I will..."

Hannah sat up in bed, her hands throbbing. It took a moment for her to realize that there was no real pain, just a phantom from the dream.

She looked to the window and noticed the morning sun was peeking through, which she supposed was a blessing. She was shocked she had made it through the night. She had fully expected to have visitors, maybe the parents of the boys who had been attacked by the snakes. The Constable, or even Pastor Dunne. But no one had come. She stared down at her hands, making fists of them, convincing herself that the pain had only been from the dream. Once she was sure, she stared up at Old Boreas, ruffling his feathers as he stared at her, protecting her. She decided it was time to get up and make her way outside to allow Old Boreas to relieve himself.

As she opened the door, Old Boreas walked a few steps ahead of her as Hannah kept her eyes on the ground. She was looking for her snakes and was saddened to see they were not there. As Old Boreas fumbled about the yard, Hannah stared into the forest and then back toward the barn. She was surprised at just how quiet the morning seemed to be. She heard a bird singing somewhere nearby, but that was all.

When she looked toward the barn again, she saw Old Boreas perched along the few remaining pieces of firewood left over from winter. She assumed her snakes would also be somewhere nearby, maybe watching her closely. The images of the day prior with the children danced around in her mind. She could still hear their howls of pain as the snakes attacked, and she wondered if she had indeed gone too far.

Of course, you did, evil is alive within you, always was, her mother's voice screamed inside her mind. Hannah slapped and punched at her face, willing the sound away. She hated the woman's voice. She looked toward Old Boreas, pleading with him. She would much rather hear his guttural voice telling her, *"The snakes are your imps...they serve and protect you. And in this, you control them.*

Hannah smiled and walked toward him. She lowered her hand as Old Boreas pecked at her skin, a symbol that everything would be OK. This thought made Hannah very happy, and she headed back inside. She ate a small breakfast and practiced creating stronger fishing nets, but her mind was elsewhere. She felt detached from everything as she replayed the events of the previous afternoon in her head. The grocer, Pastor Dunne, the boys, wondering if the boy who had been bitten by the copperhead had survived. She thought of the sort of struggles that must come with fighting off snake venom: fever, puking, foaming at the mouth, all of it. She had heard many stories about men on the frontier who had died excruciating deaths from the bites of copperheads and rattlers.

Maybe he deserved it...smug little bastard, Hannah thought.

Out of nowhere, Hannah released a startled laugh. As she tossed down her fishing net, there was a pecking at the door. She got up and opened it, not surprised to see Old Boreas waiting there for her. When he strutted inside, she glanced outside but still did not see any sign of the snakes. She looked at the road into Trumbull, down Crow Trail, and for some reason she could not identify, it filled her with a sudden jolt of nervousness. She almost felt as if there were something down the road waiting for her, *calling* her. It was something she had never felt before. Slowly, her mouth started to water. She was not hungry, but her mind instantly went to Emma Nichols and her apple pies.

Stay away.

She turned at the sound of Old Boreas' voice. The rooster stood just behind her, looking up at her.

"Stay away?" she asked. "From what?"

There is nothing down that road for you.

She thought of the snakes with the boys again, of the odd way they had behaved, as if orchestrated by an unseen force.

"And there is something *here* for me?"

The words came out in a tremble. She realized it was the first time she had ever spoken that way to the voice coming from the rooster. Her voice had been defiant...doubtful.

There is power here for you. Surely you know that. Surely you know you are protected.

And there it was. The confirmation she needed. It had been an unspoken understanding between the two of them— her and Old Boreas. And now that it had been admitted, she felt almost freed.

"Yes," she said. "Yes, I believe I do know that."

And with that, she stepped out the door.

There was no complaint or instruction to stop from Old Boreas when she closed the door behind her. When she crossed the yard, she thought she could see the squiggling movement of snakes along the edge of her property, but was not certain, so she looked away and focused on the road ahead of her. As she started down it, she thought she understood where the sting of nervousness had come from when she spied it from her doorway. After what had happened the night before, she was sure that her eventual death would come down this road. If not at the hands of an aggrieved father who had lost his son to snakebite, then surely by someone else who knew of her darkness.

She made it down the first half of the road without incident. When the Nichols home came into view, she felt oddly safe. She looked further down Crow Trail toward town, making sure she had not overlooked some ominous threat, but saw nothing. She turned her attention back to the Nichols house and saw the youngest child sitting in the yard, playing with a ratty old doll. A large smile had been drawn on its face right below the big button eyes. As Hannah approached, the little girl looked up at her. She showed Hannah the doll and made it wave at her.

"Hello there, what's this little lady's name?" she asked, pointing to the doll.

"Scratchy," the girl said.

"She's very pretty. And so are you."

The girl said nothing at first. She smiled, though, and her cheeks grew slightly red. When she finally looked back up at Hannah, she spoke with all the absurd honesty of a child. "You're a bad lady. Mamma says so."

"Does she?"

"Uh huh. She says you're a witch—that you've been marked by the devil. She says there is something black and you're rotting like her apples. Yup, that's what she says. Daddy makes her say it."

"Do I look rotten? What do *you* think?"

"I think you're real pretty, and I like your dark dresses. But daddy says you're the devil's friend. He says you're doomed."

"Maybe I am, little one," Hannah said, staring down at the child. "Do you—"

A shrieking voice interrupted her. It came from the house as the front door flew open and Emma Nichols came rushing out. She had a hunting rifle in her hands, and though she had clearly never held it before, the weapon looked no less dangerous for it.

"Hannah!" Emma screamed.

Both Hannah and the young girl whirled around at the sound. The little girl had been so badly startled that she dropped Scratchy. Hannah was sure this was how her life would end, her entire head blown off in front of this little girl and Scratchy the doll.

"You get away from her!" Emma said. Her voice carried the feral anger of a protective mother, though there was a thin thread of fear that ran through it. "You move one inch closer to her and I'll hang you myself!"

Hannah smiled but didn't doubt it. She could feel the weight of her mortality resting between the barrels of the gun and her head. As she stared at the barrel of the rifle, the voice of Old Boreas filled her mind.

There is nothing down that road for you.

"You have to go, Hannah!" Emma screamed. "This is your last warning!"

"Go?" Hannah said. She felt something shifting inside of her, something akin to a wall crumbling somewhere deep within her bones. It was both gut-wrenching and pleasing at the same time. "Yes, I will go. But first, I am here to offer my condolences."

Emma looked confused but stood her ground. "Condolences?" Her bottom lip quivered.

Hannah imagined the woman thought she had done something terrible to her daughter. But there was confusion in that distressed face, too. Beyond that was the mercy in Emma's eyes, maybe a flicker of the teachings and ramblings of the holy book she clung so desperately to. Hannah was not sure.

"For the pies," Hannah clarified as she stepped forward. "For the fruit."

Emma Nichols looked down at her daughter and began to lower the rifle. She nodded at her and ushered her away with the waving of her free hand. "Go on and get inside. I'll be back in shortly."

The girl obediently got to her feet, taking Scratchy with her. She did not look back but headed straight inside and closed the door behind her. The moment she was gone, Emma set the rifle down on the ground and crossed her arms at her bosoms. Emma's jaws were shaking, and she kept as much distance as she could, keeping a careful eye on Hannah.

"So, you *did* curse me. You cursed my pies? Why?"

"I don't know," Hannah said, but it came out in a gasping whine, trying to swallow everything down like bitter medicine. She looked at Emma's face and felt the darkness shifting inside of her. "I mean, why not? You were so defiant with me, so like the others, but then you stand before me clinging to your Bible, imagining you are a saint? It's rot Emma, all rot."

"Hannah, do you know why I came out with this rifle? Because if I do not, my girls will tell Rube. I will be banished from my home for taking up with people like you. Banished from my children, maybe the town. That is why I am like that. I must protect myself. I wanted to help you from the time I saw you at Captain's funeral. But I must not. I hope you understand that."

Hannah shook her head and somehow managed to

squeak out a response. "People like me, huh? What about the people like you? The people of this town? People that follow a book, Emma. It's just a book of fake teachings from scholars like Pastor Dunne that has convinced you it is real. And because I don't follow those teachings; I am the devil. Coming from a man trying to steal my land."

"No there is more to it Hannah, there is darkness around you, I can feel it," Emma said as she reached out and took Hannah's hand.

Hannah stared at Emma with cold, dark eyes, her gaze never faltering. Emma stepped back. It seemed as if the fear gripping her, was irrational. As Hannah tightened her grip, Emma gasped. An image of her in the woods danced across her mind. She remembered watching Hannah on that rock and enjoying it, remembered touching herself in places she had never touched before.

Hannah smiled knowingly.

"Stop it!" Emma cried. "Just stop it."

"You claim this religion, but in the darkness, you enjoy the things I enjoy. You live a righteous life in the faces of men, but in the secrets of the darkness, you delve within the evil of this town. It is all rot, I tell you, all of it."

"I'm afraid I can be of no more help to you," Emma said. "I don't know what you want. I can pray for you. That is all I can do. Would that be OK, Hannah?"

"Keep your dirty prayers! Keep it all! But I came to tell

you that you will be of help to me. You will be of help to the both of us."

"Us?"

Hannah did not answer. Instead, she felt a thrumming sort of vibration in her bones and a crackling hiss of noise in her head. It was almost like hearing someone shrieking, but from deep down a dark well. Both things together created a physical pain within her, and it took an incredible amount of effort to even breathe. Hannah closed her eyes against it and tried to focus on the message before her.

Hannah opened her eyes, surprised to find that Emma's face was streaked with tears.

"God will see to you," Emma said. "Just trust in that."

"Dear, there is no God. It is just a pile of men convincing you to believe in something that is no more worthy than a dog. Trust in that. They do not allow anything different. They do not allow a woman to think for herself, have her own wants, her own lusts, or her own devils."

Emma noticed Hannah's eyes shift as the wind picked up slightly. It was warm, but a cold chill landed on Emma's skin. She inhaled quickly but could not release it under Hannah's watchful gaze. The images of the woods appeared again as the whispers landed in her ears.

Emma! Touch yourself, Emma!

Emma trembled as the taste of salty tears stung her tongue.

"Emma, are you OK?" Hannah asked, placing her hand

on the woman's shoulder. Emma did not answer. Instead, she turned, looking all around. The whispers were still there, but now they seemed muffled, like thunder in the distance. Her eyes widened as a dark void stretched through her bones. She wanted to run, but her mind would not obey. Suddenly the ground shook, and Emma was released.

"What did you do to me?" she asked.

"Me? I did nothing," Hannah said, smiling sheepishly.

"I must go. I just must."

"Emma," Hannah said as Emma turned away from her. "I will be back."

"Just please don't come by later in the afternoons. Rube will be home, and he won't take kindly to your visiting. But if you need anything I can provide in secret, you come to me, OK? I will pray for you Hannah. I will pray the Good Lord and Our Savior has pity on you, I really will. He loves you; He loves us all. You just have to love him back."

"Ahhh, is that how it works? Of course, Emma." Hannah said with a smile.

"OK. And remember, you stay away from that town. They will be coming for you. The church has banished you, that is church law. Rube says so. They just have not decided yet. Just stay away."

"Church law?" A slight giggle escaped from Hannah's mouth. "To hell with church law. Damn it all." Hannah said and turned away triumphant—humbled in equal measure.

Old Boreas provided the security she needed. She felt protected and free. When she reached the road and turned to head home, she watched as Emma opened her door to head back inside. The little girl was standing there, waiting. And when she saw that Hannah was leaving, she held Scratchy up and made it wave again.

Hannah waved back just as Emma closed the door.

CHAPTER 27

There was not a single Bible in the cabin. After Captain died, Hannah had burned them all. She believed that too many people used the Bible as a tool to not only get out of it what they needed, but to also influence others to believe in something that they would not otherwise believe in. Like pressuring them, using it perfectly as a shield. She remembered how Captain had forced her many nights to listen to the Scriptures he read. She felt her skin burning, almost melting as he rejoiced in the gospel and the accounts of Jesus' ministry and the miraculous stories about Noah and Jonah and the great fish.

But in the hours following her conversation with Emma Nichols, Hannah found herself wondering what it was about all those old pages that had convinced so many that this was the right religion, and the only way people should think. She supposed, in some way, that was exactly what it was: a written word of encouragement that gave people something to believe in. She could not fathom such nonsense. She figured it was nothing more than a condonation and false hope.

She began to tidy up the cabin just to clear her mind, to occupy her hands, and calm her errant thoughts. She made the bed, making a note to wash the sheets with the next cleaning. She scrubbed the cabin's windows and wiped down the counter. She had started sweeping the floors when she noticed her snakes. They were coiled up comfortably in the corner of the kitchen. This made her smile and made her feel somewhat whole.

She ignored them as she completed her sweeping but felt their eyes on her. She was quite sure she could *hear* them as well. It was a muttering sound, like a broken breeze stirring dead leaves in her head, whispering.

As she moved to the pantry to place the broom back in its place, she heard the all-too-familiar tapping at the front door. Her mind felt at ease. As she opened the door, she looked down, and Old Boreas stared up at her with wishful eyes. A flash of movement startled her. Old Boreas fluttered toward her, and she stepped back, surprised at his appearance. He seemed to have grown a bit since this morning. In fact, he looked quite plump somehow, much more defined and muscular. He stood there, framed in the doorway, cawing at her. His screams were almost thunderous as he spread his wings again and gazed up at her.

"Boreas, come in," Hannah said, reaching down for the rooster. But he stepped back and pecked toward her, almost grazing her skin. Hannah jumped in amazement and continued to stare at her rooster. "Well, aren't you going to come in?"

No. Come outside, Hannah. Come to me.

Hannah did not think his voice had ever been so clear. It was like having a gentleman in the cabin, standing directly beside her, and speaking softly into her ear. It sent a delicious chill down her back, and for a moment, she felt as if some physical presence was pushing against her, trying to guide her out the door.

Old Boreas did not wait for confirmation. He simply turned on his thin legs and made his way off the porch. Something about the way he was moving unnerved her, setting off a wave of tension inside of her stomach. She followed him, though, because it would be stupid of her to overlook the now obvious things she knew about him. She was coming to understand that something was different about him. Perhaps it was something dark—a darkness that Hannah enjoyed and accepted. Then something else jogged her mind. She thought about the people of Trumbull. Maybe they were right; maybe she had been sleeping with the darkness, a darkness that she accepted and honored.

But as for Old Boreas, she also knew that there was a power within him, a strong power she had tasted and experienced. It was a power that protected her and tasted so sweet to her tongue, to her soul, that it almost made up for every day of her marriage to Captain, when she had felt so powerless. The power was beautiful. Old Boreas was beautiful. She knew right then that she never wanted to be without him.

She followed him off the porch and down across her yard. She was not surprised to see him cross over into the tree line, nor was she surprised when she saw numerous snakes slithering out of their way to grant them passage. She counted six, but there were certainly more within the grouping of intertwined bodies.

Old Boreas led her down a familiar little trail in the forest floor that had become her footpath down to the river and what she now thought of as her fishing rock. When they came to the river and he hopped up on her rock, there was a dizzying moment where his shadow was cast across the granite. It was not the shadow of a rooster, but of something much larger. Whatever it was, it appeared to have massive shoulders and at least eight appendages. It was big and alive, and it seemed to seep into every nook and cranny of the forest. The shape breathed and squirmed, its edges moving in shadow even when the rooster stayed mostly stationary.

When Old Boreas turned to look at her, she felt it in her

gut. It was like being hit by a bolt of lightning at first, but it gradually faded into something warm and encouraging. She ached in a pleasant way, a tingle of sensation that ran like a current between her brain and her womanhood.

Why are you trying to stray? Old Boreas asked.

"Stray?"

The Nichols woman. She invoked the name of the Lord. She invoked the name of prayer upon you. And you sought it. You desired it. You thought of it. I felt it.

"Prayer?" Hannah said, lowering her head, not wanting to see what Old Boreas had become. And the word came out like a fragile seed, taken by the wind and cast onto uncaring ground. She was almost afraid to speak to him, especially after having seen that shadow on the rock. Hannah felt a tender touch lift her chin, it reminded her of Captain after a firm slap to her cheek when he explained how disobedient she had become.

"Why are you—" she began, but Old Boreas interrupted her.

Aye, but you excite me, Hannah.

Suddenly, Hannah realized that she was finding it hard to breathe. It was almost as if Boreas had started squeezing the world in from all sides, robbing the forest of its air. Hannah thought the trees were going to bend and snap all around her. She searched for the shadow around Old Boreas but could no longer see any sign of the sinister shape. She knew it had

243

something to do with this suffocating feeling. She knew she had been defiant.

Do you not like the power I have given you?

"Yes." It was an easy answer, and it came to her even before she opened her mouth.

Will you allow me to continue living in your presence? Will you obey?

"I will."

Will you let them fear you?

She heard her own voice coming out of her mouth, and it was like a song. The feeling of a current passing through every fiber of her body nearly brought her to her knees. Her brain felt light and airy. She grew incredibly wet between her legs. She moaned and reeled, wanting to fall to the ground completely but, at the same time, wanting to keep her eyes on Old Boreas.

"Why have you come to me?" she asked.

You called for me and I came.

"I called?"

All the insipid prayers have muddied your memories, little girl. Even from your childhood, all the prayers and the presence of their Lord. I was weak then, as were you, in your pain and doubts, in the shadow of your fervent and disease-ridden mother. I did that, you asked me to. When she reached for you when death came calling, I was there with you. And when you were playing around the encampment with the bones of men. I am here for you, Hannah. I have always been with you. Even with Captain. Your prayers of pain to me were answered. I saw you so sad, so weak. But now, that is no more.

"Yes," Hannah whispered.

She fell forward slightly to her knees, reaching out for him, begging for his touch, his security. She spread her arms wide, and the rooster lowered his head as if in prayer. The shadow appeared again, radiating out of Old Boreas. It was wide and dark, encompassing the entire fishing rock, then the river, then the forest beyond. It grew and grew until it seemed to devour everything around her, and she felt its inky tendrils working their way into her mind.

And then, in what felt like a perverse and passionate act, it moved in and captured Hannah's soul. She saw images of fires burning on Crow Trail. Pastor Dunne came into focus. Whispers filled her ears.

Four.

Three.

Two.

One.

Pastor Dunne was standing in the middle of her yard holding something. She saw destruction and blood inside of her cabin. As she watched, the darkness left and headed toward Wayman's Gorge and into town. The images disappeared, melting like lava in her mind. The numbers escaped her lips as she counted them in sync. *Four, three, two, one.* Hannah furrowed her brow as she watched the darkness moved swiftly out of view. She slowed her breathing and stared at Old Boreas. He cawed at her, fluttered his wings, and jumped off the rock. As Hannah got to her feet, she patted his head and followed him thinking of the gift he just gave her as they walked slowly back through the forest to their cabin.

CHAPTER 28

Hannah arrived back home feeling as if she had gone out into the woods to rid her body of all its excesses. Sweat, grime, fecal matter, even the very oil of her skin, it all seemed to be gone, utterly stripped away. She walked as if she were twenty pounds lighter, and her heartbeat like a new creature inside of her chest. She hesitated on the front porch. Her hand was on the knob, but her head was turning slowly to the road toward the Nichols place.

No. Not for you. There is nothing down that road for you, Hannah.

It was Old Boreas' voice, but it now lived inside her mind. She knew the rooster was nearby, but she could not see him. It didn't matter, not anymore. He was alive inside her, and he would always be watching her.

Hannah settled down into a chair at the kitchen table and stared at the wall. She barely moved, though her mind was alive with activity. She thought of Emma Nichols for a moment, and then her thoughts turned to Thomas and his soft touch down by the river. She thought of every person in town who had cast a frightened eye upon her, and a smile gradually started to spread across her face. Slowly, her fingers started to claw at the surface of the table, her fingernails making a scratching noise against the wood. She scratched and scratched until blood appeared in her nail beds. As she sucked them dry, she could sense something coming, something dark and untold, something that would make the terrible memories of her mother and her smashed hands seem like tales of love and fancy. She could feel it coming like a dark thunderhead on a hot summer afternoon, and something in her mind seemed to speak it into existence.

She closed her eyes for a moment, trying to focus her frantic mind on the coming darkness, but there was nothing. She saw something akin to a purple curtain, and there was something moving behind it. Something huge and unnameable, something she had sensed on occasion ever since she had allowed Old Boreas and the snakes into her life. Perhaps the shadow of Old Boreas that she had glimpsed on the fishing rock was there, but she was not sure. She was slightly disheveled, with her curls falling into her eyes, a few missing hooks on the bodice of her dress, and torn lace at her shoulder. But she listened closely. That was all she did, and then—it came.

His sweet voice, breaking through it all. Just two words, hissing like a million snakes.

Be ready, Old Boreas said.

Hannah got to her feet and walked to the front window. Even before she peered out into the late afternoon, she knew the darkness would bring her much strength. She watched as all the light disappeared, but she could hear something, too. It was the creaking of wood, the almost musical churning of a horse's feet upon the earth. Looking through the night-streaked glass, she saw a horse-drawn carriage and two men sitting on it. She tilted her head curiously and noticed it was the Constable and Pastor Dunne. Then she stretched her eyes through the darkness and saw two men walking behind the carriage. They carried flaming torches. That did not surprise her. But what did was the stench she smelled coming off them. She smelled anger on them, fury, and something like lust but much darker.

Be ready, Hannah.

She nodded to the empty house and went back to her chair, turned it around to face the door, and waited.

She listened to the passage of events through the door. She heard the final creak of the wooden carriage and the last few steps of the horse. There was a faint rustling noise. As she listened to the feet of the men touch the ground, she smiled.

She thought of Old Boreas and wished he were in the cabin at that moment but felt that he was somewhere nearby. She knew the men were here for a no-good cause, but she also knew Boreas would not let any real harm befall her.

Footsteps approached, coming up the stairs and onto the rickety old porch. She heard a male voice whisper, "You ready?"

The response was even softer. "Yeah, I guess."

There was a great deal of fear in the second voice. Hannah eyed the door and raised her brow, waiting patiently. This brought a smile to her face, and it was still there when the door was opened. It came open quickly, as if it had been shoved hard by someone with great strength.

The first man wore a look of surprise. Clearly, he had not expected the door to open so easily. He looked a bit older, maybe forty or so, with a thick brown beard and oily hair that was mostly hidden by a well-worn hat. Hannah stared them both down, capturing every curve and wrinkle on their battered faces. It took her a minute to recognize them. The older man crowded in close, trying to hide his face under his hat. But she knew who he was, and it made the moment seem more sweet, more surreal. Hannah cocked her head and smiled. It was Rube Nichols, Emma's husband. The man behind him was a bit younger, maybe in his early thirties, rail-thin, and quite handsome. Hannah was pretty sure she had seen him in town once or twice.

Rube was holding an old, scarred ax, and the younger man held a hefty-looking piece of firewood in one hand. A cord of leather was draped over his shoulders.

"Hello, gents," she said in a dry, flat voice. "I wasn't expecting company tonight." She looked at their weapons again, and her heart rested easy. She was not afraid.

Rube, who seemed to be the leader of the pair, eyed her suspiciously. He had not been expecting such a formal greeting. "Expecting it or not, we're here. And we've come to teach you a lesson."

"Is that so?" She smiled coquettishly and leaned back in her chair with her legs spread wide, eyeing each man carefully.

"Tell me Rube, does Emma know you're here?"

The look Rube cast her way was filled with hatred and fire.

The younger man stepped into the cabin and took his place beside Rube. Hannah counted—One. Two. Three. Four. The young man started swinging the wood menacingly, and it made a popping sound as he smacked it rhythmically against his palm. Hannah tilted her head to glance around them and saw Pastor Dunne standing in her yard holding a flaming torch. The Constable was leaning against the carriage, lighting a cigar. Rube turned slowly and shut the door. He fumbled with the bolt lock along the frame, and when Hanna heard it snap into place, a small giggle escaped her throat.

Rube took one large step forward. The anger in him

seemed to radiate in waves. She thought there might be fear in him as well, but not nearly as much as she could sense coming off the younger man. Still, despite his fear, Hannah watched as he spat out his words, his bottom lip quivering as he shuddered.

"S-several week-weeks ago, did you happen across a young man in the forest?" he asked. "He was fishing and said he ran into you."

Hannah smiled even wider, nodding. "Problems with your tongue, I see. But ah yes. That was my sweet Thomas. He was a—"

Hannah could see rage build up in his eyes as the man walked swiftly toward her, drew up his hand, and slapped her hard across the face. It sent her flying out of the chair in a dizzying half-spin, though Hannah did not feel the sting of it until she hit the floor. The man's slap had busted her bottom lip open, and her right cheek stung as if hornets had attacked her there. She let out a gasp, but the smile remained on her face. She slowly got to her feet, and when she faced the men, the younger one advanced, drawing the length of the wood back and hammering Hannah in the stomach. She felt her throat constrict as she emitted a painful explosion of air. Her abdomen felt as if it had broken completely apart. She fell to the ground again, gasping for air but trying desperately to laugh.

"Witch! Scarlet! Did you kill Captain? Why did you *curse* him?"

"I did no such thing." She spat blood from her lip onto the floor, very close to the younger man's boots. "Though it seems the narrative of that has been decided by the ignorant people of this town."

"And my son?" the younger man asked? "What about him? What did you do to Thomas?"

"Nothing. Nothing worse than your father sowing lies into his mind about a great God. Convincing poor Thomas that there is nothing different in this world. And if you are different, you are the devil. But didn't you know, Michael—yes, see, I know who you are, Michael. Michael Dunne. There are no devils, and I know everything about you, about you all."

Michael nervously shifted his stance, glancing at Hannah and then back at Rube.

"Look at Rube standing there," Hannah goaded. "Big man. Big bad man, attacking a helpless woman. But what he cannot do is comfort his own wife. Not the way a man should." Still on the floor, she shifted to her knees, and Rube's angry eyes met hers. "Poor Emma," she drawled. "She is so lonely and sad. Her prayers go unanswered. She sweats like a slave, and when the dust settles and the worms of men sleep, Emma lays in the darkness, trying to soothe the hunger between her legs with her own hands. That is just tragic."

Rube took one large stride forward and threw his knee into the side of Hannah's head. It felt as if little shards of glass were rattling around in her brain. But through it all, she heard *his* voice. It was just as real as the voice of Rube Nichols vilifying her in the darkness of her cabin.

Be patient.

The knee to the side of her head had sent little spirals of flickering light across Hannah's vision. But then a second one came, this time from Michael, and the world became a temporary swirl of blurred colors.

"That's for my son!" Michael yelled! "What you attempted to do with my son, is that what you want? Whore! Damn Jezebel! Well, you will receive it. From a man and not a boy."

Hannah chuckled through the world of muted shapes and colors. It sounded like gurgling muddy water. "I will be so lucky," she laughed, her teeth now lined with blood. She laughed so loudly that the earth seemed to shake. Rube looked around the room as Hannah fell back to the floor, her arms spread out on each side, like an angel. "So lucky!" she laughed.

This seemed to enrage Michael and dispel any fear that remained in him. But Rube took a single step back. Hannah knew he sensed that something was wrong. She sat up and tried again to get to her feet, but Michael Dunne clamped a powerful hand around her neck and guided her back to the floor. Hannah watched as he motioned Rube over. Lust gleamed in the young man's eyes. Rube took another step forward, and Hannah's eyes widened as she watched Michael unbutton his pants.

Rube's hand clamped down in a viselike grip on Hannah's shoulder, holding her in place. "Open up, witch. And if you try anything stupid, we'll burn your evil ridden house down with you inside. Do you believe it?"

She nodded and, without objecting, parted her lips. Her bottom lip throbbed, but the pain was quickly overwhelmed by an entirely new sensation as Michael, already fully erect, filled her mouth. Hannah had performed this act before, even on Captain, and she quite enjoyed it, often making a game of it, and learning the many ways she could make him writhe in expectation and pleasure.

But this was not like that. Michael shoved his entire length into her mouth, slamming his groin into her face. It reached the back of her throat, and she gagged. Yet when she tried to pull away, Rube was there. He had one hand on her shoulder and the other at the back of her head. She gagged, choked, and nearly puked, but managed to keep it down. She knew what these men were here for; the violent thrusting into her mouth had erased the slightest doubts she'd had. She knew what they wanted, and she knew *Old Boreas* wanted her to give it to them.

Be patient.

Hearing his sweet voice in her head made Hannah relax against the violent assault. The pain in her face and abdomen faded away, and her body relaxed, including her throat. She took Michael's penis easier now, almost willingly. He was still rough with it, and when she got accustomed to his level of violence, she did her best to return his aggressiveness. She enjoyed it, she had to. Old Boreas was egging her on.

As her body continued to relax, she applied the right sort of pressure, performing tricks she knew men enjoyed. The man moaned, and when she knew he was about to reach the end, she even cupped his buttocks and urged him on. She looked up to him, her eyes locking on his, and on occasion, her eyes drifted to the corner of her cabin, searching for the darkness she longed for.

When he spent himself, Hannah found herself gagging and almost puking again. There was blood and semen running down the side of her face, but she continued. When he tried to withdraw from her mouth, she tried to keep him there. She knew she should feel shame and rage, but instead, there was a strange sort of acceptance. She felt Rube pulling and pushing her arms, trying to pull her off Michael, but she tightened her grip on him. She wanted more.

Still swooning from his pleasure, the young man finally escaped her grip and stumbled backward, trying to regain his composure. He pulled up his trousers and stared at Hannah. Confused, Michael struggled for words as Hannah lay there, smiling blankly.

Finally, she looked at him. "So, is that it? Is that what

your religion teaches you to do to a widowed woman?" She nodded pointedly at Rube. "Is that how this works?"

"Oh, you *are* a vile witch, aren't you? A vile woman." Rube said.

"Mayhap I am." She reached up and unhooked her bustier, damp with blood and saliva, and tore it open. She grabbed the bodice of her dress and pulled harder, until it nearly ripped in half. When her breasts were exposed, she grinned at Rube and slid one of her own hands under her dress, teasing her vagina.

Rube used his fist this time. It connected squarely with her chin, and for a moment, Hannah blacked out. Barely aware of what was happening, she felt Rube's hands on her, grabbing at her breasts violently. She felt him biting them, a sensation that was painful at first, but then nothing more than pure pleasure. He placed one hand around her throat and used the other hand to yank his pants down. Rube slammed her head hard against the floor, and with one quick, violent motion, he forced himself inside of her.

Hannah did not fight this, either. In a dark sort of acknowledgment, there was a part of her that enjoyed it. She thought of Captain. This was nothing like the nights they spent under the moon, coupling violently like animals in complete craving of one another. No, this was hatred, lust, and revenge. Hannah erased the thought as she felt his hands around her throat, squeezing, picking her head up and slamming it into the hard floor as he thrust into her with the speed and ferocity of a dog servicing a bitch in heat.

She cried out through the haze of pain and semi-darkness as if she were relishing every moment of it.

"Yes! My God, please, more. Harder! Come on, church man I said *harder!*"

He slapped her, and as her vision blurred, she felt warm blood trickling down from her upper lip. She licked it, reveling in the abuse as he violated her. Hannah felt something shift in the room. She felt it. It was Old Boreas and the darkness she longed for—not something within her, but within the house.

Michael started walking slowly toward the front door, eyeing the house suspiciously. "Rube, we should..."

"Shut it! You had your time, let me have mine." Rube Nichols panted and grunted with each word, continuing to pin Hannah to the floor.

"*Yes!*" she bellowed. She reached up and put an arm around Rube's neck, locking eyes with him. She smiled devilishly, licking her bloodied lips, and when she saw the alarm in his face, she started to laugh, pushing her hips into the air to meet his thrusts.

Hannah flicked her eyes toward the cupboards, and they flew open, followed by the heavy iron door to the wood stove. Then the doors slammed shut of their own accord, sending a sound like thunder through the house. The commotion made

Rube stop, though he did not withdraw from her. He looked in the direction of the stove, and when he did, the chair Hannah had been sitting in when they arrived went flying across the room and smashed into pieces against the wall.

"W-what is it?" Rube asked, then tried to withdraw from Hannah's body.

But she did not let him. She clutched him tighter around the neck, using both arms now, and wrapped her legs around his lower back. She flexed, thrusting upward to meet his length. He gasped in pleasure and still tried to get up, yet he could not move. Hannah held him like a prisoner, like the way she had been held ever since Captain had died.

Suddenly she felt another shifting in the air. He was here. Old Boreas. She gloried in the sight of him standing on the table, fluttering his wings and cawing so loudly that it bounced off the walls and spiked through the men's ears. Hannah was jubilant. Her little soldier! So triumphant, so loyal!

"Rube!" Michael yelled nervously. "Let's go!"

"I can't! She won't let me... I am trapped! It's just a stupid rooster!"

Hannah laughed. "You think so? Then come on, teach me my lesson. Teach me like you taught your wife. Don't stop!" she cried. "Like you are teaching your daughters. You swine. Your poor daughters. Is that in your Good Book?"

Hannah closed her eyes, and the curtain she had seen in her mind earlier dropped away. She saw the darkness behind it, the moving, breathing darkness. It came surfing forward and encompassed everything within her—her mind, her heart, every nerve and muscle within her body.

"Teach me!" she snarled, running a hand across Rube's face as she continued to thrust upward, trying to peel his skin away in four bloody ribbons. He howled, and when he did, Michael reached for the door.

Old Boreas took flight and pecked at the young man's hand as it fell on the doorknob, making him shriek and bat at the rooster. In retaliation, Old Boreas went for his eyes. The man continued to yell, now sounding almost like a terrified little girl as one clawed talon tore just across his right eye. The howl of pain was miserable, and it caused Rube, who was still on top of Hannah, to cry out in horror.

"Let me go!" he screamed. He continued to try to get away from her, but the power that had come over her was far too much for him. Her hips were locked, and her legs were wrapped around him. "Please, let me go! I'm sorry, so sorry..."

"*Teach me more...*"

Her hands slid down his back, ripping his shirt. Then her nails dug into his skin. As if attracted by the blood, Old Boreas was there within seconds, pecking and clawing and causing Rube to shriek.

"Lord Jesus Almighty!" he cried. He had stopped trying to pull away and sagged against her. "Lord, release me from this devil!"

Hannah craned her neck upward as she brought his head toward hers.

"Didn't you know, there are no devils," she growled in a voice that in no way resembled her own. She then greedily kissed his chin and sank her teeth into his bottom lip. She bit down hard and pulled even harder. Blood began to trickle down onto her face, hot and smelling of copper.

When Rube's lip tore away with a rip that sounded remarkably like old newspaper, Hannah finally released him. He scrambled away from her, swatting at Old Boreas, who was still taking gouges out of his back. He finally pulled up his pants and nearly tripped as he and Michael escaped through the front door and ran toward Pastor Dunne.

She heard Old Boreas clucking wildly for a moment, and then the sound of all the men scurrying back to the carriage.

Hannah got up as if nothing had happened to her. She stared at Pastor Dunne from her doorway. The Constable was already reining the horses to turn around as the minister hauled himself up beside him.

As they retreated, Hannah watched as the flaming torches left a trail of fire down Crow Trail, fighting against the wind. Old Boreas stood motionless, watching them go. She was sore, her head ached, and she could still taste the seed of Michael Dunne in her mouth, along with her own blood. But in a way, Hannah did not think she had ever been more at peace in her entire life. Old Boreas strutted back toward her. Hannah leaned down and ruffled his feathers as he cawed at her.

"What took you so long, you crazy rooster?" Old Boreas looked up at her and rubbed against her leg. "Come." She turned toward the cabin and walked inside.

Before Hannah shut the door behind them, she heard whispers echoing in the distance. As they reached her. *They will be back*. Bounced through the darkness and through the forest and echoed through Hannah's mind.

CHAPTER 29

Hannah slept surprisingly well that night. She had a very vague dream about her mother and the hammer, but it was so faint that it barely even registered. When she woke the following morning, her hands did not even hurt. When she got out of bed and started making breakfast, there were no other pains either. This was not what she expected, not after the events of the previous night. She figured there would be other pains that would present themselves, but there was nothing. Swollen lips, bumps on the back of her head from where Rube had slammed her against the floor. Blackened skin around her eyes, slashes on her cheeks, something. But there was nothing. Not even her womanhood seemed to feel different.

The entire right side of her face where Michael had slapped

and bloodied her nose was soft and clear, and Hannah smiled at the thought of it all. *Some lesson*, she thought as she felt the skin around her abdomen. Not a scratch or bruise in sight. She threw a piece of wood in her hearth, to boil some water for tea. Near the table was the long piece of oak Michael Dunne had stuck her in the stomach with. She smiled and threw it in the fire as well.

"Ratbags," she whispered to Old Boreas, who was perched on the table, watching every move she made.

As the kettle spiked a whistle, Hannah watched as the steam evaporated into the air. She stared down at her hands. The pain was gone now, and her crooked bones were smooth and straight. Her healing was a gift, a gift from Old Boreas. As she made her tea, she noticed the sun peeking through the cabin windows. She walked out on the porch to watch the earth come alive. It was not quite summer yet, but the sun was already promising an intense day, bright and powerful.

She expected the Constable to come for her at any moment. Waiting on the porch for him would be an easy task. She thought of Emma Nichols, wondering if she might visit as well. Would she suspect what had happened to her husband? Hannah turned to Old Boreas. "Might not. The sins of men are covered in lies."

In response, the rooster cawed and jumped off the porch to dig for worms and his morning feast.

She sat and watched him closely for the better part of the

morning. On occasion, her eyes glanced down Crow Trail, but no one ever came. Old Boreas continued to strut in the yard, going back and forth from the porch to the edge of the forest. Hannah eyed him and noticed there was something different about him. Something mystical, maybe undiluted. But she watched him anyway.

Boreas was fluttering his wings toward her as he stopped near the center of the yard. He tilted his head inquisitively, stared at her for a moment, then walked back near the forest. She did not hear him; he did not speak. But she was still aware of the connection between them. She could sense him, feel him. He would be with her always. She could sense him buzzing, a sort of silence, something peaceful and dark, like hibernating in some underground cavern, miles beneath her feet.

Old Boreas eventually cawed at her, and she got up and followed him into the forest. She was not sure where he was going or what he was up to, but she knew she should follow him anyway. Maybe she could go down to the river and sit on her rock. Being out there with Old Boreas, in a place of solitude, would help heal her mind. The events of last night still lingered in her brain, and she wondered what fate she would face for it all. Perhaps the natural sunlight, the intoxicating smells, and sights of the forest would rid her thoughts of the evils of this world. The sunlight poured through the canopy of trees overhead. Hannah tilted her head back, her face taking in the heat of its warmth. It was beautiful. Spinning and singing, she cherished it. Cherished it all.

She quickened her pace and made her way to the river, her arms slightly outstretched to touch every tree she passed. Their feeling on her fingertips was all the confirmation she needed: This was where she was supposed to be.

Once she climbed on her rock, she sat with her legs crossed. For a moment, it felt as if she had taken her place on a throne. She recalled the shadow she had seen on it just the day before, that otherworldly shape that had both terrified and fascinated her, and it made the rock feel even more welcoming.

Hannah felt so much stillness boiling from within. It seemed so natural, warm, and honest. At one point she looked down at her skin, rubbing her arms, expecting it to melt away like a spermaceti candle she had left in the sun. But it didn't. Her skin was soft and unscathed, and she felt it—the power of nature. She felt every tree, every insect, every bird, and everything hidden underground. She got the odd sense that, in some way, she owned it. It was connected to her.

Slowly, Old Boreas crawled in her lap, and she started to feel overwhelmed. Maybe she was not supposed to be here at all. She had been sitting there for what seemed to her an eternity when Old Boreas jumped down and stared at her. She noticed those little glistening planets swirling around in his eyes.

Come, come to me!

His voice trailed through her head like wind. It was gentle and demanding but, most importantly, reassuring.

Hannah got down from her rock and walked. She knew where to go, though she did not know her destination. It was as if the forest was guiding her. She could almost see small avenues and bends among the trees, the light spilling through the branches signaling where she needed to turn.

She walked that way for nearly half an hour, then came to a stop. She didn't know why, but her knees locked up and she *knew* this was where he wanted her. It was an unremarkable little stretch of woodland, just like every other wooded acre around the town of Trumbull. She had come through a small patch of thick vines and prickly briars, but those were behind her now. She looked back toward them and felt as if she were intruding.

Hannah!

A voice echoed from the canyon that sat before her. She was at Wayman's Gorge. Hannah walked slowly toward the massive drop in the ground ahead of her. It looked almost like a giant mouth, open and ready to devour everything in its way. Hannah peered down. She remembered Captain, on occasion, would tell her many stories about the ruins of Indian villages down there, and how, before the town was properly settled, some hunters had fallen right down into the mouth of the darkness. It was the same place where Captain had met his fate. A young deer hunter had seen his body lying at the bottom.

Hannah smiled, resting her hands calmly on her hips. The wind picked up, and a violent gust blew behind her. Her hair, which was laying perfectly like a black cowl around her face, blew up and slapped at her cheeks. The bottom of her mourning dress flared out around her, and she nodded in approval.

"Shall we think of him, Hannah?"

She inhaled abruptly and wheeled around at the sound of the voice. Standing a few yards behind her was a man she had never seen before. At first, she assumed him to be a preacher because of the way he was dressed. Thick black shirt with a black vest over it. His pants were also black, as were his boots. It all looked well-polished and quite plain. His face was somehow perfect, as if expertly sculpted by an artist. She imagined it must have been what the face of an angel looked like. His deep brown eyes regarded her politely, and when his lips curved up into a small smile, Hannah was filled with a flush of heat.

"Excuse me?"

"I asked if we should think of him. I mean, does a man not deserve some sort of souvenir. Or was he so vile, he deserves not?"

The man took a step closer, and there was something familiar about him. Not his smile, not his eyes, but...

something. "The famous Captain Hovey," he said. "A man that everyone cherished...except his wife."

It was the voice. She recognized the voice. And with that recognition came a sensation of falling while staying in place. Falling, yet knowing she was safe and protected.

"Old Boreas?" Hannah whispered.

"Silly, silly Hannah." He said walking closer, shaking his long pointy finger toward her. "Is Boreas not nothing more than a rooster?"

Hannah remained silent for a moment. "He's-he's something more to me."

"Mayhap. But that is not why I am here. The stench of men is why *I* am here, is it not?"

Something Old Boreas had told her while out on her rock came speeding back through her mind like a windstorm.

You called for me and I came.

"Yes. I came, Hannah," the man said, moving closer to her. Hannah lowered her head and noticed that the once polished garments he was wearing seconds ago had turned to nothing more than dusty cloth. But that was not what really caught her attention. It was his voice. A voice as sweet as honey and very desirous. When he reached for her hand, she gave it to him freely. When she felt his touch, she experienced love and affection like never before.

The man squeezed her hands, and Hannah saw an image of her mother. She was holding the hammer, bringing it up and smashing it down on her hands. There had been nothing but fury in her mother's face and afterward, when she had done her best to mend Hannah's hands, she laughed. Hannah saw herself kneeling at her cot and remembered praying—not to the God everyone adores, not the one her mother prayed to, but to something else. To *anything else.*

"You prayed to the bones of men. You prayed to me, and I came. Did I not?" the man asked, still squeezing her hand.

"Did I not come for your mother, for Captain? The beloved Captain Hovey, who everyone adored. He took walks on Sunday and claimed the sins of men on Mondays. The vile children causing suffrage to you. When you thirsted for the touch of men against your skin, did I not satisfy you? I came, Hannah, I gave you security, protection, and power. I came, my child, and I shall not leave."

Hannah closed her eyes for a moment, taking in everything the man was telling her. She felt stunned and satisfied at the same time as the rush of memories played out like a picture book in her mind.

"I wanted *them* to suffer. *All* of them. For *her* to suffer." The words came easily, as smooth as silk. Her body relaxed. The darkness inside of her spread, breathed, and cascaded along like waves on a dark and infinite shore.

"As she did, Hannah. I answered you and all your prayers. Her skin boiled, her body was eaten with disease. She was talking to imps, devils, demons... Legions to the serpent. She prayed to me."

Hannah nodded. She sensed the memories, but they were faint and very hazy, lurking somewhere behind that growing darkness in her mind. The man smiled, and Hannah felt herself melting, giving in, and it was blissful. But at the core of it was a very real fear. She had managed to block out the sight of her mother, sweating and screaming, feverish and half-mad as she yelled about damnation and the stench of sulfur. She had ranted and raved about a man standing at the end of her cot, a man with a sweet voice and the glowing mark of the beast.

Hannah had never even considered that such a fate had befallen her mother because of the angry prayer she had made to whatever vengeful forces that might be listening out in the night. But now, she was glad.

"But you are not like your mother, or the people of this earth," the man said. "Your mind is ripe, as is your heart. Still...they desire you, and you must give them what they want."

Hannah finally spoke. "One day."

"No, Hannah. Soon. You have lived your life beautifully. You have served yourself well. You have planted a seed of fear and doubt in the people of this town. I feel it...their faith, slipping away like maggots. I feel their terror and taste the nightmares of their children. And it will go on forever.

Your name and what you have done will be cemented for generations."

He tilted his head and considered her for a moment, then reached out and caressed her chin. His touch was cold, but she wanted it everywhere. There was no denying that. Hannah closed her eyes and reveled in the moment of solitude. A cold chill spread from her thighs and throughout the rest of her body. When she opened her eyes, the man tilted his head and released a fiendish laugh.

"Oh, Hannah. My sweet Hannah. You know of this? You have sensed it, too, yes?"

She nodded. Yes, she had. She felt their fear, tasted their doubts, devoured their insecurities, and gloried in their curiosity and lusts. She had tasted it all in the air when she had passed through their streets, their town, the fragile little shell of their filthy lives.

"They have succumbed to their greed, their desires, their hunger against sin, but it only made them yearn for the darkness. And now, you will die for it. And it shall be soon. Hannah, it will not be an easy death. But better things wait for you beyond this world. Beyond this...*veil.*"

Slowly, he released her chin. Her heart raced and something deep down ached for him. It was his voice, his sweet voice, a voice as sweet as honey—assuring her and comforting her. As silence fell between them, a flurry of information settled into her mind. She analyzed it all and, even though it worried her, it all made sense. Hannah inhaled softly and smiled at him.

"You need not worry, my sweet Hannah. "The things beyond here waiting for you will come quickly, and despite what they teach in old books and come out of the mouths of maggots, there are no devils."

These words settled over Hannah as she watched the man walk away. It looked as if the forest greeted him, almost *absorbing* him. He released himself into the woods, and the trees received him. As he walked, he left something in his wake. Hannah watched them fall, black and soft, floating down to the forest floor. First one, then another and another, settling on the ground as the man morphed into ash.

Hannah walked closer. The wind rushed in, and black rooster feathers trailed through the forest, following the man.

"Old Boreas?" Hannah whispered. Her eyes danced against the sunlight as she turned smiling walking back through the forest, heading to her cabin.

CHAPTER 30

Hannah was surprised she had made it through another night without any visitors coming to her home. She was also surprised to find when she opened her eyes, she could not remember one of the dreams she usually had when the sun fell behind the moon and the darkness filled her room. There were no creeping memories of her mother, Captain, or baffling thoughts about Thomas down by the river. Today she felt as though she'd had the best sleep of her life.

Old Boreas was perched on the end of her bed, and that brought her great comfort. She vividly remembered the man in the forest from the day prior, and the reality of her life that he had shown her. She knew she had a big day ahead of her. Thinking of it made a dark churning burst inside, but then it rested comfortably, sitting deep down in her gut. As she got out of bed and moved throughout the cabin, thinking of that darkness, she started to understand that it was something she could bring to the surface if she wanted—and, more importantly, something *Boreas* could bring whenever he chose to do so.

The rooster went to the door and started pecking. Hannah ventured toward him and stared down at him with a new understanding of their connection. She bent down and fluffed his head, and Boreas gave her a soft jab on her arm in return. Hannah opened the door, and the rooster strutted off the porch and headed straight toward the forest. Hannah watched her snakes, smiling as they slithered right behind him in what she thought was a coordinated motion.

While her eyes were cast into the forest, watching Boreas, something inside of her yearned for something else. As her eyes searched the yard, they stopped on a familiar stretch of the road, Crow Trail. She looked at it almost longingly and thought of Emma.

There's nothing down that road for you, Hannah! Boreas spoke.

"There is one thing!" she whispered softly as she walked off the porch and into the yard.

Rocks and stones cut at her feet as she walked the road that led her to Emma Nichols' house. She could hear subtle movement in the woods to her side, and she knew it was Old

Boreas, escorting her along the way, keeping a low profile under the brush. She had learned early on that if he didn't want to be seen, he would not be. But knowing he was there gave Hannah a sense of contentment.

She stopped in front of the Nichols house and stared at it for a moment. She could hear the ghosts of Emma Nichols' voice, offering prayer over her. It felt like nails in her head and termites crawling on her skin. She thought of pies made with rotten apples, the worms in them that would never die, and stepped into the Nichols's' yard.

The girls were around back, laughing and singing. She heard them so clearly. Their youthful voices, so innocent, waiting to be corroded by the teaching of a godless world and the likings of men.

> *"Goosey, goosey, gander,*
> *Whither dost thou wander?*
> *Upstairs and downstairs*
> *And in my lady's chamber.*
>
> *There I met an old man*
> *Who wouldn't say his prayers;*
> *So I took an ax,*
> *And hit him in the head!"*

Hannah approached the front porch as the girls brought the song to a close. One of the girls started to laugh hysterically.

"That's not how it goes," the other screamed.

Hannah smiled and knocked on the door. She knew Rube was not home, she felt it, she sensed it. She was here for a reason—something brought her here.

As Hannah assumed, Emma Nichols answered the door. She was wearing a black house dress. This made Hannah chuckle inside. She had never seen Emma in black before. She wondered if Trumbull had lost another swine. She knew better, though. She would have smelled it. The dress was wet around the top and center. A little speckle of soap suds on her forearms made Hannah think the woman had been doing the wash when she knocked.

"Hannah, are you OK?"

"Emma? I—" Hannah stopped, her eyes growing narrow and dark.

Emma shook her head slowly and took a step back. Her hand went to the door, but she did not close it.

"Come down," Hannah said. "Let's go down, down the stairs and off the porch."

Emma nodded anxiously and folded her arms in front of her. Hannah took a few steps back, and Emma followed slowly. As she drew closer to Hannah, something stiffened inside of her, and her breath seemed to be suspended. Far beyond her reach of sight, Emma felt something lurking, watching her. It felt evil.

"You told me to come to you whenever I needed anything."

"That I did, and it still holds true. But like this...you seem different."

"Different?"

"Just more alive. No longer frightened, I guess. Your face... it's just different. But what is it you need?" Emma asked.

"There were two men that came by the house," Hannah said. "They said they were there to teach me a lesson." Hannah went on, "But it was more than a beating. They...they took me as a man would take his wife and by other ways."

"Hannah," Emma grinned. "Beating? But you look as though you are...well perfect. What do you mean, a beating?" she asked, staring—absorbing every inch of Hannah's face.

"I cannot explain that Emma, but they violated me."

Emma shook her head. "I don't need to hear more of that. Do you need help, the Constable maybe?

"No! I just need you to know. They are coming for me Emma, and I need you..."

Emma interrupted. "Why have you come to me with this? I can pray for you. Do you want prayer, Hannah?

The voice that escaped Emma's mouth was not her own. It was sweet, sweet as honey to Hannah's ears, and she thought of Old Boreas out in the forest. Her heart surged at the thought of him, and she stared malevolently toward Emma Nichols. There was a bit of shame in it, but it was fleeting.

"There are things I need to tell you," Hannah said. "I need you to share a message with the townsfolk when I'm dead."

"Hannah, you don't need to die."

The words went through Hannah like nothing more than a breeze. She barely heard them. They meant nothing.

Hannah then slowly pulled out the thread of information she had been given in the forest. She heard it all in her head as if coming from the voice of Old Boreas—which she now knew beyond any doubt was the same as the voice of the man from the forest.

"My body cannot be burned. It must be carried to a grave like any other resident of Trumbull. And I should not be buried near a church, but out in the woods, near living, moving water. And it must be after—"

"Hannah, you're talking cra—"

"Silence, woman!" The voice that came out of Hannah's mouth was maniacal. It was the sound of ancient doors closing against old stone frames, of forgotten bodies screaming, lumbering about in rotting tombs.

Emma Nichols reeled, and tears sprang to her eyes. Her face flushed, and her skin tightened, but she nodded toward Hannah. She was too scared to retreat inside or cast her eyes away at that point. It seemed the voice that had come from Hannah had clued her in to the authenticity of her instructions.

"I cannot be buried before sundown," Hannah said. "It must be under the light of the moon. And my body must be taken by hand, not by cart."

She stopped here and found that once she had spoken these instructions, her body felt immeasurably lighter. She felt like she could float away if she wanted to.

Emma could not look directly at Hannah—she did not want to. Her sobs were still apparent, but they grew to a howling scream. "How do you know?"

Hannah shook her head slowly and began walking away. She walked backward, keeping her eyes on Emma while the sound of the children singing once again reached her ears.

"Accept it, Emma. Accept things you shall never understand. Accept it all."

"Hannah, how?" Emma yelled.

"I think you already know."

As Hannah turned and started her journey back to her cabin. Emma stood silent as she watched Hannah twirl and spin down the road, humming. Echoes of the forest sang in sync landing clearly in Emma Nichols' mind.

CHAPTER 31

Night had fallen.

Hannah stayed awake for as long as she could, but eventually dozed off. She woke up several times thinking she had heard footsteps, but the only true noise came from the slow and methodical steps of Old Boreas out in the kitchen. Hannah found herself habitually running her fingers over the backs of her hands, missing the lumps and small scars, the misshapen bones from when her hands had healed improperly as a child.

When she opened her eyes and finally found that the sun had risen, she counted it as a blessing. Only, as she opened the front door and allowed the sun to wash over her, it was not the God of Emma Nichols' devotion that she thanked for this additional time. Instead, she thought of the man down in the woods. And thinking of him, she drew Old Boreas close to her side.

Hannah did not eat at all that day. She barely sipped some water, but only because her body seemed to demand it. She spent most of the day sitting on the porch or inside at her kitchen table. The table had not been cleaned in several weeks. It was littered with crumbs and countless snips of fishing line and netting where she had continued to practice her knots. The little books she had used to learn the craft were tattered and well-worn somewhere underneath it all.

How silly, Hannah thought, *that I once worried over such trivial things.*

She thought about the man in the woods again, about Boreas and how he had told her that there were things waiting for her beyond this veil. She did not know what that meant, exactly, but she believed it. She believed it just as much as others in town believed every word jotted down in that holy book of theirs—the book they used to justify all their wrongs and misdeeds while also helping to make them feel special.

The day wore down and, as evening approached, Old Boreas walked over to the front door and asked to be let out by pecking at it. When she opened the door for him, the rooster peered out, making a very strange sound as he extended his head outward. Hannah could not help but wonder if the creature was somehow sniffing the air.

He slowly walked outside, strutted down the stairs and

then stopped. He seemed to be staring out toward the road, unmoving. It told Hannah everything she needed to know and, somehow, she was not frightened. In fact, she left her front door open when she went back into the house. She sat down on her kitchen chair, pointed it toward the open door, and waited.

They came about an hour after nightfall.

They were not quiet about their intentions at all, the light from the torches was visible in the darkness, and the sounds of their footfalls on the dirt road were like thunder. As they came into view, Hannah could see the dust they were kicking up illuminated in their torchlight. It looked like a series of rampant phantoms skirting along the road.

And still, she did not move. She sat on her chair and watched them draw closer until their shadows reached her lawn. Slowly, Hannah stood up and walked out onto the porch. The crowd stopped when they saw her, and a hush fell upon them. Hannah guessed their number to be twenty or twenty-five, depending on how many cowards were lurking near the back of the mob. She could hear some people murmuring; she heard one woman's voice muttering the Lord's Prayer. Hannah noted that a few of the men in the crowd held pitchforks, but more notable than that was the fat man near the front. He held up a noose, as if making sure Hannah could see it.

Hannah stepped slowly across the porch, down the stairs and into the yard, and a nervous little ripple of movement passed through the crowd. She had no problem accepting this fate and started to wonder what other fruits waited for her beyond this life, beyond this *veil.* She wondered who might be there, waiting for her.

As she stepped toward the crowd, arms held out to her sides, palms facing up, Hannah noticed the line of fire that seemed to go for a mile down Crow Trail, their torches burning bright.

"You just stop right there, witch!" the fat man with the noose said.

Another man, wearing a small silver emblem on his chest, angled himself out toward the front of the group. It was the Constable, followed by Pastor Dunne, then Rube Nichols. The Constable looked to a man standing to his right holding a pitchfork, and then to the man with the noose.

"Do you accept this fate, woman?" Pastor Dunne shouted. "You have been found guilty of witchery and laying with the devil."

"Guilty, without a trial. And you call yourselves men of God!" Hannah shouted back. She walked closer, eyeing the crowd. She smiled toward Rube, expelling saliva from her mouth and spat at his feet. Rube stared back at her, his anger turning to fear as she edged closer to them.

"And where is this God you speak of? Hannah yelled. Pastor Dunne stepped back. Inhaling swiftly, shouting the words of blasphemy, roaring up the crowd.

"She killed Captain!" a woman in a long gray dress shouted.

"She seduced my Thomas, made him swallow the devil's juice!" Michael Dunne screamed.

Hannah laughed staring curiously towards him. "Yes, as I have swallowed yours!"

"Lies from the devil." Pastor Dunne yelled! The crowd cheered, waving their torches toward the darkened sky.

"Made my boy's skin boil! He's resting well with the Lord now."

"As is mine. Devoured by her snakes. Serpents of the devil."

Hannah stood silent. As the screams flew toward her like the musket rounds Captain once used, she ignored it all. Six of them came forward right away, flanked by the Constable and Pastor Dunne. Another half dozen followed, aiming their torches toward her. Hannah stepped forward and noticed a small object standing before her. It was Old Boreas.

He had gone unseen in the darkness and was looking directly at Hannah, seemingly unconcerned with the mob behind him. He fluttered his wings and cawed at her, strutting rapidly behind Hannah, where he stood triumphant.

Not for you.

A warm gust of wind flushed out from behind her. As it tickled her skin, prickles of hair rose on the nape of her neck. Hannah smiled. She watched as the torches sparked a trail of fire down Crow Trail, and into the forest. She shut her eyes and inhaled slowly through her nostrils, feeling the presence of safety behind her. It was someone she knew and someone she accepted. It was Old Boreas, her protector. Hannah felt her body shiver and she felt at peace. The same feeling, she had encountered in the woods near Wayman's Gorge.

"This is not for you, Hannah! I shall not allow them to scorn you! The men of God, the men of sin!" he whispered to her in the veil of the breeze. *"Just accept it, accept it all. Do not fear them, these maggots of bones."*

Hannah complied. She walked closer to the mob; her arms stretched out like an angel. She stared into the crowd, tracing each of them with her eyes. With each step, a painful pinching sensation fell along her feet. She yelped slightly but did not show fear. It was the copperhead, the one that brought her the rabbits to feast upon. Now he was there, coiling back upon itself, getting ready to lash her again. In the soft light of the approaching torches, Hannah could see the twin pinpricks at the top of her foot, dripping blood. Just as her eyes fell on that, the sensation came again. This time it was higher up, on her left calf. She cringed against the pain and stumbled a bit but found solidarity.

It came twice more in rapid succession, all on the back

of her leg. She fell to her knees, silent as her head tilted back, staring at the night sky. *Open your eyes, Hannah,* Old Boreas said. *I am here, with you forever!* As Hannah lowered her head and looked back into the crowd, they watched in shock. Snakes from all through the countryside had appeared, and there were writhing masses of them all around her. Hannah stared into the eyes of Rube Nichols as she fell forward into the serpents, her arms open wide like a mother preparing to embrace her children. And she smiled.

Hannah felt only one more snakebite on the side of her neck before everything went numb. She could feel the venom inside of her, rushing like a living spring. It thrummed and sang, tickling and electrifying her. She craned her head to look at the crowd and saw that they had all stopped. The fat man with the noose was backing up, his eyes alight with horror. The Constable looked like he had seen some monstrous creature from the bowels of the earth, his eyes wide and alight in the torches as they lit up the night.

The fat man backed into one of the men carrying a torch and they both went to the ground. The Constable let out a tiny squawk when Hannah laughed maniacally, as it was her final command.

Old Boreas jumped on her chest, jabbing her neck, cawing toward the crowd as the torch hit the ground and sparks and flames trailed toward her cabin and the grass that surrounded it. She saw the flames leap and jump toward the crowd, climbing up the pants worn by the Constable and Pastor Dunne and trailing along the road, into town, toward the church.

To Hannah, the fires were little more than small, glowing specks in a field of comforting darkness. She heard none of the screams or commotion taking place less than ten feet away from her. All she heard were incomplete prayers, flesh sizzling, and voices that had once besmirched her name begging for mercy that was not coming.

She felt the snakes writhing around her and, for a moment, it felt as if they were carrying her on their backs. She no longer felt the ground, just the snakes beneath her as their venom washed through her and cleaned her out. Hannah watched as Old Boreas strutted in front of her, like the little soldier he always was. She used her last breath to smile because she felt herself being spread about, passed around among the snakes and into the air, into the forest all around her. She was floating, vibrating, and it felt like she was flying.

In the final moment, she heard the flutter of ruffled wings as a familiar rooster let her know that in the place beyond this one, she would not be alone.

Hannah reached for him as she closed her eyes, drifting off into some other place. As the screams of the others became more apparent, they were brutal at first, but eventually waned away until it was almost like music. The world ebbed, flowed, and burned around her, but all Hannah could feel was that place beyond this one, pulling her forward, and it felt like an old lover calling her home.

CHAPTER 32

Emma Nichols had seen the crowd going by her house. Knowing that Rube was among them made her uneasy. She had been tending to his wounds over the last few days, injuries he claimed he got from a rogue bear while out in the woods two days prior, but she didn't believe a word of it. After Hannah had come by, detailing an attack at her cabin, it had made her wonder, and now, she wasn't sure what had happened to him. What she did know was that she had felt something like a cold cloud envelop their home ever since he had come home bleeding and terrified.

Now he was out there with that frenzied crowd, heading to the house at the end of Crow Trail. Emma whispered a series of prayers softly and quickly. She prayed for the people of Trumbull, for Rube, and for an end to all of the hatred that had settled in their hearts, but most of all, she prayed for Hannah. She remembered their last conversation, and she was certain that Hannah had known what was to be. She supposed God would forgive them, though. He would forgive them all. They were, after all, going after an imp of the evil one that Pastor Dunne preached about on Sunday mornings. She wondered if the pastor was to blame. Maybe Hannah was right, maybe he was the cause of all of this, twisting the words of the Good Book to benefit his teachings. She wasn't sure, but something about it all just made her wonder.

Emma got up from the kitchen table and checked on her daughters. The younger one was in bed, almost asleep. The older one was stitching up one of her dresses by the light of a lantern.

"I'm headed out for a bit," Emma said. "Look after your sister, would you? I won't be long."

"Yes ma'am," her eldest said, having no real clue of what was taking place in the darkness not far from her house.

Emma went to the bedroom and slipped her shoes on. Before leaving the room, she placed her hand warmly and lovingly on the family Bible that sat on her dresser. She hurried out of the house and, not wanting Rube to see that she had joined the mob, stuck to the woods. She wasn't sure why she was even going out. Morbid curiosity, she supposed. But something seemed to be tugging at her, even calling her, maybe.

Emma made her way through the forest, holding her lantern out directly in front of her. Right away, she noticed sparks flying up in the distance, lighting up the night. As she hurried her step, a few low-hanging limbs swatted her face, and one even tugged at her hair, spiraling it out of the tight bun that sat gently on top of her head. On a few occasions, she thought she saw a deer moving through the woods to her left, farther away from the road, but when she looked out into that darkness, there was nothing there. That's what her eyes told her, anyway. Her heart told her otherwise, and she found herself still praying, praying against anything moving along with her out there in the darkness.

Up ahead, following the line of the forest, Emma halted briefly when she realized she could see Hannah's cabin. Through the shrubs and trees, she saw the flames flickering against the night sky. She watched as the cabin burned rapidly. The crowd stood motionless a few feet away. Emma strained her eyes through the darkness when she noticed something else in the yard, something breathing or moving or...

It was a rooster. She saw him strut quickly across the road and disappear into the forest across the way to Hannah's house. Emma couldn't help but smile as she watched him march the way he did. Then she saw Hugh Smith with a noose in his hand, backing up directly into a slim fellow with a torch, a man that Emma did not recognize. She watched in horror as they both went down, and the fire seemed to come alive the moment it touched the ground.

It climbed up the leg of Reginald Hudson, igniting in a way Emma had never seen fire behave before. Reginald began to scream like a panicked woman as he tried batting the flames, but then his arm lit up as well. The wavering flames jumped to the man beside Reginald. It seemed to be alive and seeking anyone who had harmed Hannah. Emma could not see him, so she did not know who it was, but it was the most horrifying sight she had ever seen. She watched the flames devour his shirt and consume his face. When he screamed, it was like the fire was coming from inside of him, highlighting his teeth and the cavern of his throat. She could see the dark opening of his mouth through the bright flames, and it made her take a stumbling step backward. She thought she was staring into the mouth of darkness.

Emma placed a hand to her mouth, aghast at what she was seeing. Even now, from a good distance away and hidden by the trees, the smell of burning flesh tickled her nostrils. She stood stoically, watching the flesh of men burn away like wax. With her mouth agape and nerves buzzing like bees in her stomach, she started to pray. She prayed that peace would come to all of them. But as everything caught fire, moving swiftly, trailing down the road, it was like watching little tongues of fire dance upon the night.

Most of all, she prayed for Hannah. She prayed the

woman would survive the vile lashing that was brought upon her, and she prayed for the judgments, all of the eyes that had fallen upon Hannah after Captain died. Emma prayed for it all. But as the crackling noise of the fire consumed everything in its path, she knew better. She lowered her head in defeat, as she felt a soft tear escaped her eye as she lifted her hand up over her mouth to mask the stench of the burning flesh. The smell was awful, and the sound of the screams that echoed through Trumbull that night was something she was sure she would never forget.

When the fire jumped and began to follow a path down Crow Trail toward the town, Emma inhaled quickly and thought of her children. As she turned to run, something stopped her. It was a voice, a voice that spoke to her from a place of darkness. A voice so sweet, she thought it reminded her of honey.

CHAPTER 33

Emma Nichols tried to pass on everything Hannah had told her. As Emma spoke the instructions to Rube, it all fell on deaf ears. And Emma, in return, received the beating of her life for associating with such a god-less, devil woman. Rube refused and simply was never able to admit his wife had any sort of relationship with the woman—not after the way the night of her death had unfolded. In the end, eleven of the twenty-seven people who had marched out to Hannah's house had died. Nine had been burned alive, including the Constable and Pastor Dunne. One was trampled to death, and one other had died of snakebites. The town doctor reported that the poor fellow had been bitten eleven times by copperheads.

She never had a chance to tell the undertaker about

Hannah's burial instructions. Rube forced her into secrecy. She did, however, watch as four men carried Hannah's body down the road, away from the destruction and into town. Her cabin had burned to the ground along with the barn and anything that breathed life on the property. The church was nothing more than dust and ash along with most of the businesses in Trumbull. It was as if the grocer's, the bank, and the mercantile store had never existed.

They were carrying her body on a small stretcher made from wood poles and old canvas. According to Rube, the town would not allow a carriage to be used, as they felt it was too extravagant for a witch who had caused so much turmoil in their town. But because of old-time superstitions, and a bit of respect for the deceased Captain Hovey, they supposed she was due *some* sort of burial...just in case.

As they passed by her home with the shape of Hannah on the rickety stretcher, a chill passed over Emma, and she knew she had made a mistake. She was damned now. Perhaps they all were. Maybe it was due to their sins, or maybe it was for ridding the town of the likes of that mean old witch, Hannah Crannah, she was not sure.

She heard her daughters laughing and chasing something on the side of her house. She walked around to see what the girls were playing with. As she turned the corner, she saw them holding hands and making a circle around something sitting perfectly still in the grass.

"Girls, whatcha got there?" Emma asked, walking slowly toward them. She spied the creature resting comfortably at their feet.

"It's a rooster, mama. We found him this morning."

"A rooster, huh?"

"Yup!" the youngest one said happily. "And his name is Old Boreas. And he says he will be with us forever." As she spoke these words, she jumped up and down in delight.

"Old Boreas? That is a strange name, don't you think?"

The girls laughed. "Welp, that's his name. He told us so."

"He did, did he? Well, don't let your father see him, or that bird will be on the dinner table tonight," Emma said. She turned and made her way back inside. She figured she would try to make some pies, maybe whole cakes for the week.

Rube was sitting in his rocker, smoking a pipe, and having a nip of whiskey. Emma had stayed clear of him since the incident with Hannah. Her blackened eyes wore the effects of his rage, and sometimes her womanhood felt as though it was being ripped out each time he forced himself on her. Now he let out a tired sigh as he began to sharpen the blade of his ax.

"That godless woman was laid to rest today. You hear of it?"

"No, but I saw the four men hauling her off."

Rube nodded. "They put her out in the Four Corners, near Captain. You know the open field out there? Captain deserved better."

Emma did know what he meant. There was an old field that was covered in trees and shrubs on the edge of town. Some folks referred to it as the waste grounds, where derelicts and stragglers lived. Hannah was placed near the mud-ridden road for all to see. *A reminder*, Emma thought, for the darkness that moved into the town of Trumbull.

In her mind, Emma replayed Hannah's instructions. *By hand, not in a carriage, somewhere in the woods near moving water, by the light of the moon.* Emma was reminded of it over and over.

Emma set her last pie on the windowsill above her wash pan and stared out into the yard. The rooster that the girls had been playing with earlier was standing under the massive oak near the road, tilting his head and eyeing her cautiously.

"The town is better off now that she's gone," Rube said, moving into the kitchen. He laid his ax on the table and walked near the sink.

"Yeah, I guess," Emma whispered, her eyes still focused on the black rooster standing in triumph in her yard. Suddenly she felt a sting on the back of her head as Rube slapped her back to reality. The tears came freely and rolled down Emma's cheek.

"Speak, woman. What is wrong with you?" he screamed as he sat at the table again, nipping at his whiskey.

The rooster cawed toward Emma, rustling his feathers. Images of Rube danced in her mind. She saw him violating

Hannah in her cabin. As the image morphed into dust, it was replaced with Emma's youngest daughter in her room sleeping in her bed with Rube standing over her, unbuttoning his trousers. She wiped her hands with a cloth that was spread out over her sink, then walked toward the table near Rube. She felt comfort all around her, almost as if a cloak had been wrapped around all her fears and they were all being removed from the world that Emma once knew. She felt whole and protected, finally at peace.

"A godly community like this has no room for evil like that...no room for *devils* like that," he said.

Emma stared toward the window as the whispers were being driven in by force. She stared at the ax and back at Rube. Her hands quickly picked it up, and with one violent swing, she drove it down into his skull. As Emma watched the warm blood trickle down his head and into his eyes, she smiled.

Emma leaned in closely, shrugged, and whispered,

Don't you know... There are no devils.

AFTERWORD

I hope you have enjoyed the Legend of Hannah Cranna, The Witch of Monroe. Although this book is a work of fiction and is not in no way intended to be depicted as Historical Fiction, Hannah Cranna was a real person.

Hannah's grave is very easy to find—right on the hillside in the front of Gregory Four Corners Cemetery in Trumbull, Connecticut. Her final resting place overlooks the road with a bright white headstone to this day. It is marked "HANNAH CRANNA" and not her Christian name of Hannah Hovey.

Some claim that Hannah was a warrior for women's rights in a time when such matters did not exist. From many stories recorded about her, it is said she was a very strong and an unruly woman that was not to be messed with. She grew up around witchcraft and was seen on many occasions with her familiar Old Boreas, talking to him.

For more information about the real life and death of Hannah and Old Boreas, please visit:

The New England Historical Society or Gregory Four Corner for more information.

For other books by Trace Murillo, please visit www.tracemurillo.com.

ACKNOWLEDGMENTS

There are a few people I would like to thank while writing this book.

As always I want to thank my husband Shannon for his undying support for everything I do. For putting up with my many hours of ignoring him while I wrote this book and understanding why.

All my children, there are too many to name but one, Joshua Murillo for your love of history and guiding me on many late nights about how the force of religion can damage so many souls. A tip of the hat to him for his insights and suggestions.

A profound and heartfelt thanks to T.W. Robinson, a fellow writer, for guiding me through and introducing me to so many in this business. You sir are an inspiration.

To Eleanor Ransburg. A woman that has dedicated her life to guiding children but still made time to edit this book. I thank you!

To my readers, I thank you for allowing me into your life if only for a moment. To share my work with you, is honestly the highlight of my career.

Jennifer McElroy, you are my rock. My advisor and confidant. I appreciate you more than you will ever know.

To Emily from Emily's World of Design for a terrific jacket design and Adam Gaffen for helping me find her. I thank you both.

To Lady Madia Codd for guiding through the dark places of demonology that allowed me to create such inspiring characters. Your logic allowed me to have an open mind and made me rethink everything I have been taught. For that, I thank you.

A special thanks to the New England Historical Society for the information on Hannah Cranna and the injustice so many suffered in this time due to the Christian Orthodoxy that was forced on them.

ABOUT THE AUTHOR

TRACE MURILLO was born in Florida in 1968, the youngest of eight children. She currently lives in North Carolina with her husband and her dogs. She enjoys traveling while doing research and has seen some amazing things and has met some great people along the way. Trace is an avid reader and book collector of the classics and hopes to have her own library one day. She loves books! Any books, but normally, horror, thrillers, or the supernatural are her favorites.

When she is not behind her computer writing, she enjoys cooking and baking. She enjoys long hikes near the Blue Ridge Mountains and takes semi-horrible pictures of the scenery. In her down time, she watches many classic cult films. She is currently working on a psychological thriller, *Whispering Creek,* due out next year.

Visit Her Online
Web: www.tracemurillo.com
Facebook: facebook.com/tracemurillo

www.ingramcontent.com/pod-product-compliance
Lightning Source LLC
Chambersburg PA
CBHW021313250626
47155CB00002B/513